DESIGN FOR LOVING

Returning from holiday, Katie Mead discovers her business partner, Jack, has apparently vanished into thin air and a mysterious stranger, Lyall Travis, is lodging with her Aunt Alice . . . Despite reservations, Katie accepts Lyall's offer of help with her forthcoming jewellery exhibition. Theirs is a stormy relationship, for she suspects he was involved in Jack's disappearance. Katie enjoys Lyall's company, but her emotions must be kept in check until she has discovered the truth.

JEAN M. LONG

DESIGN FOR LOVING

Complete and Unabridged

LINFORD
Leicester

First published in Great Britain in 2005

First Linford Edition
published 2006

British Library CIP Data

Long, Jean M.
   Design for loving.—Large print ed.—
Linford romance library
1. Love stories
2. Large type books
I. Title
823.9'14 [F]

ISBN 1–84617–341–8

Published by
F. A. Thorpe (Publishing)
Anstey, Leicestershire

Set by Words & Graphics Ltd.
Anstey, Leicestershire
Printed and bound in Great Britain by
T. J. International Ltd., Padstow, Cornwall

This book is printed on acid-free pape

1

Whistling to herself, Katie Mead turned the corner leading to the workshop. Refreshed from a fortnight's holiday, she was raring to get on with designing her jewellery. The tune died on her lips, however, as she saw the white Peugeot pulled up in the courtyard. Either Jack had come into a fortune or they had an early morning visitor.

The workshop door was wide open and she dashed inside, eager to discover what was going on. 'Jack!'

But the man rummaging through the cupboards wasn't Jack and, in a fleeting moment, as he turned to face her, she registered that he was tall and muscular with longish fair hair framing his tanned, handsome face.

'Who on earth are you?' she challenged.

The man surveyed her slowly, taking in the shapely figure in jeans and sweatshirt, the clear skin and silky dark-brown hair scraped carelessly back in a scrunchie.

'I could ask you the same, but I assume you're Katherine Mead.'

Katie, feeling at a disadvantage, drew herself up to her full height of five feet four inches and met the piercing hazel eyes with a cold stare.

'What if I am? You're trespassing . . . Where's Jack?'

His expression was stern and there was a determined set to his squarish jaw-line. 'If we knew that I wouldn't be here at all. I wondered when you'd show up, heard you were back last night.' He extended his hand. 'Lyall Travis. I'm staying at Mrs Mason's.'

'Well, that's easy enough to check out,' Katie told him ignoring the hand. She reached for the phone.

'She's away,' he informed her. 'Her sister was taken ill soon after my arrival, so I'm taking care of things until she gets back. I've moved into the flat.'

Katie glared at him, her topaz blue eyes full of disbelief. 'She would have let me know!'

'She didn't want to spoil your holiday so she left a letter for you. You can always verify it, ring her at her sister's. In the meantime, I'm afraid Jack's cleared off and, apparently, taken most of your stuff with him.'

She gave a little laugh, 'That's ludicrous, Jack wouldn't have done that.'

'Well, I can assure you he has!'

Katie fixed him with a scathing gaze, convinced that, for some reason, he had a grudge against Jack and was doing his utmost to blacken her friend's character.

There was a stony silence and then he said, 'If you don't believe me, why don't you ask Shelley?'

'Shelley!' Rather belatedly, Katie remembered the third member of their team. 'Where is she?'

'Oh, she'll be along presently. I told

her I'd take a look round, try to see what I could make of the situation.'

With an effort, Katie pulled herself together. 'So what makes you feel you've to take charge of things here? How do I know Jack isn't lying in a ditch somewhere and that you're not the one who's made off with all our things?'

The minute the words were out of her mouth she could have bitten her tongue, for she realised she could be dealing with an armed robber, although, somehow she didn't feel threatened, just angry at his ridiculous accusations against Jack.

He shrugged. 'Believe what you will. The fact remains that what I'm telling you is true. Search my car if you like, but you won't find anything. Look, I don't want to worry Alice Mason with all this, she's got enough to think about at present. She's obviously fond of Jack and treats him as if he were her own nephew.'

Katie's mouth was dry and she

swallowed. 'Yes, well she hasn't many relations of her own, so she was naturally over the moon when Jack turned up about ten months ago, after her late husband's solicitor finally managed to track him down. She'll be devastated if what you say is true. I expect it's all a silly misunderstanding.'

But Lyall Travis looked serious enough and, for the first time she felt uncertain. 'I suggest you take a look in the safe, Miss Mead and see if your things are there.'

Her topaz eyes smouldered. 'Oh, I wasn't born yesterday, that must be the oldest trick in the book. What a smooth con artist you are!'

'Please yourself,' he told her angrily. 'I've got better things to do with my time than argue with you. I'll be outside if you need me.'

Katie locked the door behind her and went into the back room. At first glance there was no sign that anything had been disturbed. She sighed with relief as she looked through the drawers where they kept their tools and found them all intact.

On opening the cupboards a moment later, however, her worst fears were realised, for the boxes that had housed their work had been removed. Shelley had obviously discovered this already, but didn't have the combination to the safe where Katie had stowed away a number of the more expensive pieces of jewellery for their exhibition.

Heart in mouth, she hurried over to it now and keyed in the numbers. The heavy door swung open beneath her touch and, removing one of the cases, she opened it to find just two pairs of earrings and a note from Jack. It was an I.O.U. together with the words: SORRY KATIE. I HAD NO OPTION. I HOPE YOU'LL FORGIVE ME.

In a daze, she relocked the safe and sank down on to a stool, burying her head in her hands. All she could think about was the exhibition in London in a few weeks' time and that all their hard work had been for nothing.

As for Jack, none of it made sense. She couldn't imagine what would have possessed him to have behaved like that. She had thought the three of them had a good working relationship, but she had obviously been mistaken. Relief surged through her, as she suddenly remembered that she had placed some of the valuable items of her silver jewellery in a safety deposit box at the bank, prior to going on holiday.

Lyall Travis was sitting on the old mounting block in the courtyard. 'Well?'

She shook her head in bewilderment, wondering just exactly who he was and if she could trust him. 'I don't understand what it's all about, but Jack seems to have let us down big time. We're supposed to be exhibiting in London in a few weeks' time and, like you said, he's disappeared with most of our stock.' She swallowed. 'I apologise for doubting you. I don't know how you've come to be involved or why. You're not the police, are you?'

His eyes flickered. 'No, just a concerned bystander. I told you, I've taken the flat in Mrs Mason's house. Shelley came to me for help when Jack took off on Saturday. I didn't think you'd want the police brought in, but perhaps I was wrong.'

She shook her head. 'No, I need to work out what's happened first.'

He jumped athletically off his perch and caught her arm. 'Come on, let's have some coffee and talk about this in a civilised fashion.'

It felt as though his fingers were burning into her flesh as, against her better judgement, she allowed him to lead her back into the workshop.

A few minutes later they sat at one of the workbenches sipping steaming mugs of coffee.

'OK, so let's discuss the situation. Jack's let you down badly. I suppose we can assume that he intends to sell your jewellery?'

She nodded. 'He's probably already done so over the internet. We've recently got our own web site. Unfortunately, it gets worse ... He's also walked off with my supply of silver. However, looking on the brighter side, he's left our tools and I've still got some of the larger pieces of jewellery, for the exhibition, on deposit in the bank.'

'He couldn't have taken those?'

She shook her head. 'He didn't know they were there. I usually keep them at home, but being away ... ' An awful thought suddenly struck her. 'Of course, he could have emptied our business account because he was a signatory! I'll have to go to the bank and find out, and I also need to see Shelley, discover just how much of her enamel work he's taken.'

'Quite a bit, from what I gather. She was too upset to say much yesterday. So, without Jack you can't go ahead with the exhibition?'

She sighed. 'No, I'm afraid it just wouldn't be possible. The three of us joined forces about ten months ago,

and, although our work is very individual, we made a good team. We need
three displays in order to satisfy the
entry conditions. Jack's a very talented
potter and has obviously taken the best
of his own stuff with him, as well as
ours.'

Lyall Travis sat back on the stool,
hands cupped round the mug of coffee,
a thoughtful expression on his handsome face. He looked up. 'Would you
consider a substitute?'

Katie was startled. 'What do you
mean?'

'Well, I'm a bit of an artist myself.
Perhaps I could help.'

She stared at him, wondering if he
were serious. 'You? It's kind of you, but
I don't think paintings would fit in with
our theme.'

He waved a hand at her impatiently.
'Just hold on a minute! Let me explain
what I had in mind. Ceramics, bowls,
coasters, cufflinks, that sort of thing.'

Everything was happening too quickly,
and suddenly Katie, still confused by

the morning's events, was full of doubts. Had she been mad to confide in this stranger?

'Wait a minute. How do I know you're genuine?' she challenged and watched his face darken in sudden anger.

'I thought we'd already had that conversation. I can provide you with references if necessary.' He got to his feet, pushing the stool back with a clatter. 'Think what you choose to . . . but, just remember one thing, you might not find anyone else who is prepared to offer help at short notice in order to bail you out of this disastrous situation!' And, throwing Shelley's keys on the table, he strode out of the building.

Katie, aware that she'd probably jeopardised their only chance of help, wondered if she would regret her hasty words. A visit to the bank did nothing to reassure her either.

She had just returned to her cottage when Shelley arrived. 'I've just heard you're back! Oh, Katie, whatever are we going to do?'

Katie, who wasn't at all clear on this point herself, gave her friend a hug. 'Jack's virtually emptied our bank account into the bargain. I just wish I knew what had possessed him.'

'It's all my fault,' Shelley moaned, sinking on to the nearest chair.

'Yours? How do you make that out?'

The girl looked distraught. 'I saw what he did and didn't try to stop him. He persuaded me that he needed our stuff to take up to London. Said the organisers of the exhibition wanted to know what the standard was like. Katie I'm so sorry.'

Shelley was as pretty as a picture, but rather scatty and incredibly naïve. Katie hadn't the heart to be angry with her.

'He's been through some of my things here too, hasn't he, Shelley?' she said quietly. 'You were supposed to be keeping an eye on the house. One or two things appear to have been moved. I was so tired when I got in last night that I didn't notice. In fact I've only just found Aunt Alice's note amongst the junk mail.'

Shelley looked embarrassed. 'He came round with me the morning he left, said you'd want him to take the best of your jewellery, along with mine, to give the right impression, and did I know where you kept it, but of course I didn't. So he opened one or two drawers. He seemed annoyed because your bureau was locked. Katie, he seemed so different, so unlike himself, but I didn't guess what he was going to do or I'd have tried to stop him.'

Katie sighed, realising it would be useless to be cross with the girl. 'Well, fortunately there was nothing he could get his hands on here.'

'I'm glad Jack didn't get those beautiful necklaces. Where are they?'

'In the bank, of course. I wouldn't have been so stupid as to have left them lying about the place, although in the heat of the moment I thought I had. He must have got the combination to the safe somehow. Probably by watching me and memorising it. Anyway, what about you? I suppose all your lovely enamel work has gone, too?'

Shelley's enormous blue eyes filled with tears. 'Most of it! What are we going to do, Katie? I can't possibly ask my family for any more money. I've borrowed enough off them as it is.'

Katie patted the younger girl's shoulder. 'Don't worry we'll think of something.' She was tempted to tell Shelley about Lyall Travis' proposal, but didn't want to raise her hopes until she'd thought it through properly. Anyway, he'd more than likely changed his mind by now.

'Of course, the immediate problem is capital so that we can start building up our stock again. The bank aren't prepared to help and, I have to tell you, it's highly unlikely we'll be able to claim on insurance, because Jack had his own key to the workshop. In any case, I really don't want to involve the police in this, do you?'

Shelley shook her head, blonde curls bouncing.

Katie got to her feet. 'Well, in the meantime, I'm going to see the Glovers and see if we can, at least, postpone paying the rent for a couple of weeks until we get back on our feet again.'

A few minutes later, Katie walked along the picturesque street towards the gift shop and tearooms, sandwiched between cottages with window boxes spilling over with Busy Lizzies and trailing Petunias. Her friend, Faye Glover, who owned the workshop premises, looked up and smiled as she opened the door. Apart from two elderly ladies lingering over an early cream tea, the place was deserted which meant Faye would have time for a chat.

'Katie, did you have a wonderful time? Have you had lunch?'

Katie, whose mind had been on other things, shook her head. 'I'm not hungry.'

'Nonsense!' Faye called out to her husband, Dylan, as he emerged from the kitchen and he disappeared again. Katie knew that if anyone could put things in perspective for her, it would be Faye. She sat on the chair opposite Katie, pushed back her mop of unruly auburn curls and said, 'OK, so how was it?'

'Fine,' Katie told her honestly. 'Of course, it would have been better if Pete had been there, but it wasn't to be and I'm getting used to being without him.'

Faye gave her an old fashioned look which spoke volumes. 'He wasn't right for you, Luv, but I can understand how devastated you must have felt when he . . . '

'Dumped me. I'm over it, Faye. It's been almost two years now and it's time I got my life back together again. Actually, I thought that's what I was doing, but now it's happening all over again.'

'Jack? Shelley told me,' she added, seeing Katie's surprised glance.

Katie nodded. 'Not that there was anything serious between Jack and myself, but I found him good company and we did go out now and again.'

'And you've absolutely no idea where he's gone?'

'None. Your guess is as good as mine. Of course, he's made off with all our stuff for the exhibition and our entire bank balance. I tell a lie, he's left us enough to pay you a week's rent.'

Faye whistled. 'Well let's hope he had a very good reason!'

Dylan Glover reappeared and set down a loaded plate in front of Katie, on which was a fluffy ham and cheese omelette, salad and buttered toast.

'You're spoiling me, but it looks good.' She tucked in, her appetite suddenly restored.

Faye and Dylan were a thoroughly nice couple, who had been good friends to Katie during the eighteen months she had lived in Lyndhurst.

They fired questions at her now about her holiday in Yorkshire, visiting friends, obviously trying to take her mind off other matters for a few minutes.

'Have you met this new lodger of Mrs Mason's?' Dylan asked.

'Yes, he was at the workshop this morning and I was hoping you could tell me a bit about him.'

'Can't help you there, I'm afraid. He arrived shortly after you went away and he's renting the flat from her on a temporary basis. Mrs Mason must trust him or she wouldn't have left him in charge of the house.'

'He's rather dishy, isn't he?' Faye put in, watching closely for her friend's reaction.

Katie concentrated on her omelette. 'Is he? I haven't noticed.'

Just as Katie was about to broach the subject of the rent, Faye, said, as if reading her thoughts 'Katie, you're not to worry about the workshop rent for the time being. Now, there's to be no arguments. It's the least we can do in the circumstances. Wait until you're solvent again and then we'll set up a new contract.'

Relief was written all over Katie's

face. 'I don't know what I've done to deserve such good friends. Thank you! You've taken a load off my mind. I was wondering where to find the money to buy some more materials. Jack's taken practically everything. Poor Shelley's devastated.'

Faye looked sympathetic. 'I'm not surprised. You've both worked so hard. Mrs Mason will be upset when she finds out what Jack's done, too. She thought the world of him. So you say Lyall Travis was at the workshop this morning?'

'And he seems to think he can fill Jack's place. Apparently, he's an aspiring artist — dabbles in ceramics.' She told her friend of the offer he had made.

Faye's eyes widened. 'Then I'd go for it, if I were you. After all, you haven't really got anything to lose, have you?'

'But, I've only known the man for five minutes!' Katie protested.

'And exactly how long had you known Jack, before you took him on board?'

'That was different, he's Aunt Alice's nephew,' Katie said defensively.

'By marriage,' Faye pointed out. 'Anyway, how exactly did that benefit you in the light of recent events?'

Katie coloured slightly. 'I'm sure there's a perfectly logical explanation for what's happened. Jack'll be back. It's just a momentary blip.'

Faye sighed. 'Come on, Katie, I know that's what you'd like to believe, but, deep down, I think you know Jack's gone for good. Dylan had a look round the bed-sit yesterday and it would seem he's made off with a few items from there too, a kettle and such-like.'

* * *

Returning to Lavender Cottage, Katie did what she ought to have done several hours back, picked up the phone and dialled the contact number on Alice Mason's note. Shortly afterwards, feeling much happier, she went into the kitchen and put on the kettle for some tea.

Her old friend had managed to reassure her about Lyall Travis. Apparently, many years back, he and his family had stayed with Aunt Alice and her husband, who had a thriving bed and breakfast business in those days. Lyall had always meant to look her up again and so, while visiting friends in Sevenoaks, had called in on the off chance that she still lived in Lyndhurst.

When he discovered that she had a flat to let, he decided to stay for a few months, as he was in between jobs and liked the area. There were still a lot of unanswered questions and Katie was not sure if she should put her faith in a man she had only just met, but what other option had she got?

2

That evening Aunt Alice's cat, Sheba, discovered Katie had returned home. They shared a tin of tuna and then the little animal curled up contentedly on Katie's lap. While she was poring over the accounts, trying to assess their financial situation, there was a knock at the door.

Lyall Travis stood on the step. 'Mrs Mason's cat seems to have disappeared, and as I've promised to keep an eye on her, I'm feeling rather responsible. I don't suppose . . . ?'

Sheba chose to put in an appearance at that moment, purring loudly. He grinned and bent to stroke the sleek, grey fur. 'Well, that solves that problem. I take it you're old friends?'

'Certainly are. Look you'd better come in. I wanted to have a word with you, anyway. I found Mrs Mason's letter mixed up in a pile of junk mail. Now that I've had a chance to read it and speak with her, things are much clearer. I'm sorry for doubting your word, but it's all been a bit of a shock.'

Showing him into the cosy little sitting-room, she hurriedly scooped up the papers from the coffee table not wanting to divulge too much about her business affairs in one go.

He perched on the edge of the sofa. 'So we're calling a truce, are we? You've obviously decided I haven't bumped all your friends off after all, and that I'm not about to make off with the family silver.'

'Your choice of words could have been better,' she told him severely.

He grinned, revealing a dimple in his chin. 'Sorry! Now, if we want to be ready for this exhibition, we're going to have to get a move on, aren't we?'

'Agreed. So we might as well discuss things in a civilised manner.'

Going over to the sideboard, Katie fetched a couple of glasses and a bottle of wine and handed him the bottle opener. Placing a dish of nuts and raisins in front of him on the coffee table, she said, 'Of course, there is one thing we've overlooked, your name isn't on the entry form.'

He gave her a glass of wine and sat back on the sofa, looking completely at ease. 'Oh, no problem, that's just a formality! I can deal with it if you'll let me have the details. Now Shelley is raring to get on with her enamelling, so I've told her that just as soon as I get the go ahead from you, I'll go up to London and get all our stuff from my usual suppliers and put it on my account for the time-being.'

Katie gaped at him. 'You seem to have taken an awful lot upon yourself. I'm not quite penniless and I would have found a way to help Shelley out somehow.'

'Yes, I'm aware that you're very independent, but the question is, can you afford to be? Look, why don't you let me put some money into the business short term? I've been looking for a new investment anyway.'

She gasped. 'Why would you want to do that, when you don't know anything about us?'

He raised his eyebrows. 'That's not strictly true. Remember, I had the opportunity to speak with Mrs Mason for a few days before her sister was taken ill. And, of course, I met Jack and Shelley, and was shown round the workshop before things took a downward spiral. You've got a thriving little enterprise there, Miss Mead.'

'Did have, you mean.' Katie was uncomfortably aware that the man sitting opposite her had somehow managed to edge his way into her life before she had fully grasped what was happening. Shelley was obviously under his spell and he had managed to charm both Faye and Aunt Alice. Katie still found herself suspecting that he might have an ulterior motive.

Lyall Travis gave her a dazzling smile.

'Come on, Miss Mead. Why are you still hesitating?'

She toyed with the stem of her glass. 'Just because Shelley is young and gullible, it doesn't mean to say that I am.'

His amused gaze swept over her. 'Come on, you're not that old. Late twenties, I'd say.'

Katie glowered at him. 'You've been questioning Aunt Alice!'

He chuckled. 'I told you we'd had a chat, but you needn't worry, she's very discreet and didn't give any of your innermost secrets away.'

Katie wondered how much Aunt Alice had told him. Had she mentioned Katie's own reasons for being in Lyndhurst, her broken engagement to Peter, and her need to find somewhere quiet to sort herself out? She sincerely hoped not. 'So what exactly did she tell you?'

He helped himself to a handful of nuts and raisins. 'Oh let me think now! She outlined the set up at the workshop, told me how Jack had been part of your team for the best part of a year and that, although he was her late husband's nephew, due to a family rift she'd not set eyes on him since he was a little boy. I don't know any details, but I gather she's been generous to him since he's been here.'

'I don't know what you're implying, Mr Travis!' Katie told him angrily. 'Jack was always kind to her and she enjoyed his company.'

The man opposite her spread his hands and sighed. 'Alice Mason is an astute lady who is fully aware of Jack's failings. I expect she is also aware that you had feelings for him, and didn't want to disillusion you.'

Katie refilled their glasses, as the impact of his words hit her. Had she been too blind to see what was going on under her very nose? Was she such a poor judge of men that she couldn't tell whether or not they were being sincere? First Peter, and now Jack had let her down.

There was a silence, and then Lyall Travis said, 'You still haven't given me an answer. Do you accept my offer to join you in your business or not?'

She considered, aware that he was watching her. 'Just tell me what's in it for you, first of all.'

'Fair enough! As Mrs Mason's probably told you, I've been abroad for the best part of a year and now I'm back in England looking for a new enterprise. Your craft venture happens to appeal to me. Ceramics have been an interest of mine for a while now and I'd enjoy helping you out for the exhibition.'

She met his hazel eyes with a penetrating blue stare. 'OK, so what do you do for a living — when you're not travelling?'

'Graphics. I work in advertising — mostly freelance.'

Her eyes widened and he saw this with amusement. She took a deep breath. 'Why on earth didn't you tell me that before? You'd be a godsend.'

He grinned. 'It was worth it to see your face. You have a very expressive face, you know. But seriously,' as she coloured, 'you didn't ask me, and, obviously, Mrs Mason hasn't mentioned it, although I suspect she's filled you in about other things.'

Katie nodded. 'Well, yes. She told me about your recent trip to Australia and how you and your family stayed with her as a child, but beyond that . . . '

Sheba appeared suddenly from behind the curtains, stretched and gave a prodigious yawn. Then she made a beeline for Lyall and jumped on his knee. He stroked the little cat under the chin as he told Katie a little bit about his work and, as she watched him, she was very aware of what a very attractive man he was — older and more mature than Jack and very self-assured.

'So what do you reckon now, Miss Katherine Mead? I have to tell you that this is the final offer.'

Katie made a rapid decision, hoping

she wouldn't regret it. 'OK, then, thanks, I accept. Of course, it's going to be tough going, to get everything assembled in such a short space of time.'

'We'll manage. As a matter of fact, I've got a few designs worked out already. Now, what about Shelley?'

'Oh, she's not likely to raise any objections . . . I've already sounded her out, and she's up for it and happy to leave the decision-making to me, although, of course, the three of us will need to have a business meeting soon to sort out the finer points.'

'Of course, and I'd like to take a look at your accounts sometime. Good, now that's settled, I'll go up to London tomorrow to collect some of the basic supplies. Perhaps you'd care to accompany me? I expect you'd prefer to get your own stuff and Shelley's?'

'We've been ordering over the internet recently, but I suppose it would be better to collect on this occasion,' she said rather hesitantly.

'Right then. I'll pick you up at around eight. We'll breakfast in London, shall we?'

'That sounds civilised!'

'I'm afraid I've got a couple of things to do in the afternoon, but I'm sure you can find something to occupy you, and then we could perhaps have an early meal before heading back here.'

She smiled at him. 'Thanks, that'd be great. Welcome to the team, Mr Travis.'

'Lyall,' he told her and, as he took her outstretched hand, a frisson shuddered down her spine.

A few minutes later he left, and she collected the glasses, her head in a spin. She wasn't usually so impetuous, but she recognised that the man had a magnetic quality about him. The sensible side of her told her to be cautious. She hadn't got a good track record where relationships were concerned and was determined not to get hurt again.

Anyway, a man as attractive as Lyall Travis, was bound to have a woman in his life. Katie picked up the phone and dialled Shelley's number.

The following morning was grey and drizzling. Katie had a coffee and croissant to keep her going, and had just finished washing up when Lyall knocked on the door.

'Did you feed Sheba and put her out?' she greeted him.

He grinned. 'But, of course. Shelley's coming over later to see to her needs, just in case we're not back.'

He picked up the post from the doormat and, as he gave it to her, his fingertips brushed hers. She wanted to gasp at the contact and bit her lip, knowing that she would have to keep a tight reign on her emotions where this man was concerned. Charming he might be but she still wasn't convinced that she could trust him.

They made good time and were soon breakfasting in a swish hotel in Kensington. Lyall looked immaculate in a grey suit, crisp white shirt, and blue silk tie. Jack had been Bohemian in dress and was often unshaven at this time in the morning. She was glad that she was wearing her new green trouser suit. She caught him looking at her and lowered her gaze, determined to keep their relationship on a strictly business-like footing.

The trip to the supplier's didn't take long, and Lyall seemed to know his way around. In a relatively short space of time everything was loaded into the boot of his car. He arranged a convenient meeting place with her for that evening and dropped her off at a nearby tube station.

She found herself wondering where he was going and wishing she could accompany him. It was a long time since she'd been in London, on anything apart from business, and she felt at a bit of a loose end. She hadn't too much money to spare, thanks to Jack, and after browsing round one or two shops, decided to go to the Victoria and Albert Museum to seek inspiration for her jewellery. She wandered happily through the costume section making notes, had a coffee and was surprised at how quickly the time passed away.

It was approaching six o'clock as she made her way to the Italian restaurant Lyall had pointed out to her that morning, but there was no sign of him. It was a chilly evening and, after a short while, she went inside and ordered a cappuccino.

The minutes ticked by and she was beginning to wonder if he had stood her up. She didn't fancy having to make her own way home and was feeling more than a little irritated when Lyall strolled through the doorway.

'Oh, here you are. How sensible of you to come inside. Had a good day?'

'You could at least apologise,' she said crossly.

'What for?' He looked genuinely surprised.

'You're late. You said you'd be here at six o'clock.'

He frowned. 'I've been stuck in a traffic jam for the past hour or so. You'll have to forgive me.' She calmed down. 'You thought I'd let you down, didn't you? You'll have to learn to trust me, Katie Mead.' He pulled out a chair, a glint of amusement in his hazel eyes. 'Right, enough of that, let's enjoy the evening. Have you decided what you'd like to eat?'

Over the pasta, which was excellent, he watched her visibly relax. He was aware of the need to tread carefully if he wanted to gain her confidence in him. He told her a little more about his trip to Australia, proving to be both an interesting and entertaining companion and, almost before she had realised it, had asked her a few pertinent questions about herself.

'So, how long have you lived in Lyndhurst?'

'For the past two years. My mother was born there and my grandmother only died six months ago, leaving me the cottage. She was a great friend of Alice Mason's, who isn't my real aunt, of course.'

'I see, and have you any other family?'

'Yes, my parents have retired to Dorset and my brother went with them, but I came to live with my grandmother because I wanted to be nearer to London.'

And, at that time to get away from Peter, she added to herself bitterly.

Lyall was asking too many questions and before she had a chance to slip in any of her own, he had skilfully brought the conversation round to Jack.

'So Alice Mason traced him through her husband's solicitor?'

'Yes, it was really quite easy. A number of years back, Uncle George had received a letter informing him that his brother had died and that his sister-in-law and her son had gone to live up north, but he hadn't attempted to get back in touch with them.

'As he got older, however, he regretted this and wanted to put matters right between them, and so, after his death, Aunt Alice decided to try to track them down. As it happened, they still used the same family solicitor in London.'

'I see,' Lyall said again and ordered dessert from a hovering waiter.

Katie tucked into the mouthwatering selection of Italian ice-cream with enjoyment. She set down her spoon. 'What I can't make out is, why Jack decided to leave whilst both Aunt Alice and myself were away.'

Lyall gave her a long look. 'Probably because he hadn't got the guts to face up to the pair of you. He told me he had a bit of history, admitted he'd got himself into debt. Personally, I reckon his past had caught up with him and he was running scared. Actually, if I hadn't been around that evening there might have been further problems.'

She went cold. 'How do you mean?'

'He came round to the house, said he'd left a couple of things in Alice Mason's safe, but, of course, I didn't fall for that one.'

'So what did you say?'

'That he'd have to wait until she returned. Of course, he didn't like it, and, as it is, I think he made off with the silver cigarette box on the hall table.'

Katie stared at him. 'Aunt Alice will be so upset. She's so fond of him. I hadn't the heart to tell her what's happened. You must think I'm a complete idiot, but I really believed in him. He was a talented potter and we were good as a team . . . Our stuff sold like hot cakes in the tea shop.'

He laughed at the pun and she joined in, relieved that it was all over.

Shortly, after more cups of cappuccino, they left the restaurant and he drove her home.

He said little during the journey and she must have drifted off because she awakened as the car pulled up outside Lavender Cottage.

'Come on, sleepy head, I'll see you to your front door. I'll bring the stock round to the workshop tomorrow morning and we'll make a start on our little enterprise.'

'That sounds good to me. Thanks for the meal, Lyall and for believing in us.'

Taking her keys from her, he opened the cottage door and turned on the light. 'All part of the service.' Catching her hand in his, he pressed it to his lips. 'Sweet dreams, Katie, I'll see you in the morning. We've an exhibition to prepare for.'

3

Katie went to the workshop early the next morning, having selected ideas from her book of designs. She had two main themes for her work, one based on leaves, flowers and fruit and the other abstract designs inspired by swirling lakes and patterns on wood bark.

Lyall was already at work and obviously in a very business-like mood.

He looked up briefly and informed her, 'Your materials are in the back, locked in the cupboard.' It was as if the previous evening had never happened.

They worked in companionable silence for a while and then Shelley turned up full of enthusiasm and bright ideas and, for the first time since her return to Lyndhurst, Katie felt a spark of interest again. It had all been so difficult during the past couple of days that she hadn't known which way to turn.

She dreaded telling Aunt Alice of Jack's departure and was putting off the evil moment. For now, however, she decided that to bury herself in her work would take her mind off things.

Katie thought that the best option would probably be to make a number of pendants and bracelets because, although earrings and rings took less time to fashion, they were quite fiddly and wouldn't take up much space in a display area. She would concentrate on the larger items first and then see what time was left.

After a while she got up to check something on the computer and discovered that she had an e-mail message. It was from Jack and had obviously been there for several days. If only she'd thought to check before.

I'M SORRY KATIE. YOU MUST BELIEVE ME. I HAD NO CHOICE. I'LL CONTACT YOU AGAIN SOON, J.

Katie made a swift decision not to tell Lyall or Shelley, wrote the message in her diary and deleted the e-mail. She was a trusting girl and was convinced, deep down, that there had to be some simple explanation for the way in which Jack had behaved.

If only he would ring and explain things then, perhaps, she could, at least, try to understand what had happened and attempt to talk things through with him.

'Are you OK, Katie?' Shelley asked in concern, as she went back into the workshop.

'Oh, I'm just a bit tired,' she replied, a shade too brightly. 'I'll put the kettle on.'

She went across to look at the designs Lyall was working on. They were certainly impressive, very colourful and professional. She could not wait to see the finished products.

Katie forced her attention back to the task in hand, knowing that she could not afford to slack, not only because of the time factor, but also because the materials were too expensive to waste.

Eventually, she lost herself in her work, which she loved, and had fashioned several items by the end of the morning.

She excused herself from joining the others for lunch, making the excuse that she had a slight headache, and returned to Lavender Cottage. The post had been and she recognised Jack's handwriting on an envelope with a frustratingly indecipherable postmark. In trepidation, she ripped it open. The message inside was brief and to the point and backed up what he had said in his e-mail.

KATIE, PLEASE DON'T THINK TOO BADLY OF ME. I'M IN TROUBLE AND NEED YOUR SUPPORT. WE'VE ALWAYS BEEN GOOD FRIENDS AND I'M SURE I CAN TRUST YOU. JACK.

Katie sat staring into space. She supposed she ought to contact the police, but what good would it do at this stage? And then there was Aunt Alice to consider.

In a way she wished Jack would make a clean break so that she could pick up the pieces and begin to get on with her life again, but he seemed intent on involving her and playing on her emotions. She could not imagine what sort of trouble he had got himself into, but it was obviously serious.

She had been sitting there for about ten minutes when there was a tap on the door. It was Lyall looking concerned and, in spite of herself, an odd little frisson danced along her spine. She longed to confide in him, ask his advice, but something made her hold back. Instead, she asked coolly, 'Aren't I allowed any peace?'

Startled, his dark eyes flashed. 'Oh, I can see you're in a mood. I just knocked to see how you were, but I know when I'm not welcome. I've brought you some lunch, but I rather wish I hadn't bothered if that's your attitude. Fine, I'll leave you in peace then!'

And, before she had a chance to say

anything, he was gone. Curiosity, made her lift the teatowel covering the tray, and she discovered one of Dylan's chicken salads neatly arranged on a plate covered with clingfilm, together with a crusty roll. She felt embarrassed at her outburst after Lyall's kindness and, surprisingly, tucked in with a healthy appetite, thoroughly enjoying the food.

After coffee, she wandered back along the lane, feeling much better equipped to face the afternoon. But Lyall was not there, only Shelley humming away to herself in the usual chaotic muddle that she liked to work in.

She looked up briefly. 'Lyall had to go into Sevenoaks for some reason. He's nice, isn't he?'

'Don't be fooled by his charm. We know very little about him.'

Shelley shot her a surprised glanced, but wisely said nothing. For some reason Katie found herself in a steaming mood and knew that it was because Lyall had gone off on a mysterious assignation, and that she had been used to Jack keeping her informed of his movements when they were working on a project.

Team work was important at times like this. She sighed, realising that she was being unreasonable. After all, Jack was hardly keeping her informed now, was he? So what did it matter?

She worked hard for the next few hours and, just as she thought they had seen the last of him for the day, Lyall reappeared. He looked appraisingly at their work and said, 'Well you two have certainly made great headway today. Now where do you suggest we keep all this?'

Katie gaped at him. 'Well in the safe, of course. Jack's hardly likely to try the same trick twice. Besides, I honestly believe he'll pay us back when he can.'

Lyall gave her a piercing look. 'Your faith in him is touching, Katie. I would hate to disillusion you, but I think you can say goodbye to any idea you might have of recompense. I've yet to find a thief who repays his victims.'

'And you know a lot of them, do you?' she asked pointedly.

'My you do have a tart tongue today!' He studied one of her pendants. 'How long do you suppose it will take you to make enough for the exhibition?'

'We'll need to work all the hours that God made in order to be ready, and that means we won't be able to keep our usual outlets supplied, so we're going to lose trade that way.'

'Have you thought about borrowing items back just for the exhibition?'

'How do you mean?' she asked, puzzled.

'Surely you must have some local customers who would be more than willing to lend you the items they've purchased. They'd probably be tickled pink to know that their jewellery was going to be exhibited.'

'But just imagine the insurance complications if we did that,' she pointed out.

He shrugged. 'It was just a thought. Was Jack in charge of organising the exhibition?'

'No, we made joint decisions on important issues. I'm still convinced there's some perfectly rational explanation for the way he's behaved. It's just so out of character, isn't it, Shelley?'

Shelley nodded. 'Seemed a decent enough bloke to me. Anyway, I've got to be off now. See you tomorrow, guys.'

For a few minutes, Lyall busied himself at the back of the workshop, but then he came and sat at the bench. 'There are one or two things we need to sort out before too long, if we're going to proceed with this project,' he told her pleasantly.

Katie set down her tools. 'Such as?'

'It all seems rather casual and haphazard here at present. I had thought there would have been more of a system.'

Katie bridled. 'How dare you come in out of the blue and start criticising.

We all got on well enough in the past. We were beginning to make a reasonable go of things.'

'Look, I don't think you can object to my making one or two suggestions for improvements, seeing as I'm putting up some money. You're hardly in any position to get uppity.'

'Meaning that if we don't go along with what you suggest, you'll withdraw your support, I suppose! Well, so far as I'm concerned you can go ahead and do just that! We'll find some other way of keeping this show on the road!'

And, sweeping up her belongings, she flounced out of the room, locked her jewellery in the safe and left the workshop, not even bothering to look in his direction again. If she had done, she might have seen that, far from being annoyed, he was grinning to himself.

★　★　★

Katie hadn't been in long when the phone rang. She picked it up and Faye's cheerful voice said, 'We're expecting you round for supper tonight, Katie.'

'You've done nothing but feed me since I've been back. It's kind of you, but I was planning to have an early night.'

'Nonsense, you've got to eat! Anyway, we've got a proposition to put to you and we'd rather tell you in person. We'll see you around seven-thirty then.'

Knowing better than to argue, Katie thanked her friend and went upstairs to get ready. She showered, changed into black trousers and a red tunic and caught back her newly-washed hair with a scrunchie.

It was only a short walk to the café. Faye greeted her warmly, apron tied about her ample waist. 'Come along in. Dylan's just sorting out some wine.'

There were four places set and, seeing her enquiring glance, Faye said, 'I've invited Lyall to join us, hope you don't mind. Oh dear, I can see from your expression that you do. Did something happen in London that I ought to know about?'

Katie shook her head, wishing she hadn't accepted the invitation. It would be awkward having to make polite conversation, after their recent heated exchange. 'Everything's just happening too quickly. I can't get my head round it. When I went away I left Jack in charge of the workshop and now he's gone and Lyall's come on the scene wanting to change everything. I don't feel as if I've had a chance to get to grips with the situation. How do I know if he's genuine?'

'Oh well, I'm sorry if I've dropped you in it. I thought you two were getting on OK. I'm being absolutely honest, though, I've got to admit that I've never really trusted Jack. He's an amiable enough character, but rather too smooth for my liking, whereas Lyall is much more straightforward.'

Katie stared at her friend in surprise. 'What makes you say that? He's an unknown quantity as far as I'm concerned. For all we know, he might have forced Jack out so that he could take his place and get his hands on our business and Aunt Alice's family heirlooms.'

Faye laughed. 'Don't be so melodramatic, Katie! You know as well as I do that Aunt Alice doesn't have any family heirlooms, otherwise why would she resort to taking in a lodger?'

'She gets lonely. She told me so. Anyway, what makes you think Lyall's any different from Jack? He's probably got his eye to the main chance too.'

Faye folded some table napkins. 'Oh, it's just an instinct. Actually, my main motive for inviting him here tonight was to see if we can find out a bit more about him. Satisfied?'

Katie, knowing that she was giving her friend a hard time, pulled herself together. 'Sorry, Faye, but you know the old saying, 'Once bitten, twice shy.' It was such a shock finding Jack gone like that. My whole world seems to have turned topsy-turvy all over again. I mean, who is Lyall and how come he turned up so conveniently? It's all such a puzzle.'

'Well, young Shelley doesn't seem to have your doubts. She's raving about him, thinks he's really talented and going places.'

Before Katie could make any comment, the doorbell rang and, a few minutes later Dylan came into the room with Lyall, who was clutching a bottle of wine. From the surprised look on his face, he hadn't expected Katie to be there either, but his greeting was friendly enough.

As usual, Dylan and Faye had surpassed themselves with the meal. The crown roast of lamb was succulent and the vegetables cooked to perfection.

After some general conversation, Faye said, 'I bet you find it strange being back in England, Lyall.'

'Yes, it's taken some getting used to. My sister tells me that my little nephew keeps asking her when I'm coming back.'

'You're an uncle?' Katie could not hide her surprise.

Lyall looked amused. 'Yes, is that so improbable?' He turned to the others. 'Katie seems to think I came down in a flying saucer on the village green and sent Jack away in my place!'

They laughed at this and Katie coloured furiously. 'Looking it at from my angle, is it any wonder that I'm so sceptical? I go off for a couple of weeks holiday, leaving Jack in charge and I return to find he's gone, Aunt Alice is away and you're here instead.'

'But I would have been here whether Alice Mason and Jack had gone away or not,' he pointed out reasonably.

Dylan carved more meat and offered it to them. When their plates were replenished, he asked casually, 'So what made you choose this neck of the woods to live in, Lyall? Why Lyndhurst?'

'Ostensibly, because I felt like a change from city life. Before going to Australia, I did freelance graphics mainly in advertising, but the company I did most of my work for has been taken over and the new people have brought most of their staff with them. Fortunately, I've still got a number of other contacts, but I fancied diversifying and so, when I learnt about Katie's business enterprise, it seemed a golden opportunity to take up my other great interest — ceramics.'

Faye cleared the plates and, a few moments later, returned with a sumptuous-looking tiramisu and some apricot tartlets.

Katie studied Lyall as he shared a joke with Dylan. If her friends were prepared to accept him, then why couldn't she?

'I've told Katie I've got a proposition to put to her,' Faye said.

Katie wished Faye would not be so open about everything in front of Lyall. She still couldn't help thinking that, somehow, there was a connection between Lyall's arrival in Lyndhurst and Jack's sudden departure. She looked up to find three pairs of eyes watching her expectantly and said brightly, 'This dessert is wonderful, Faye. OK, fire away, I'm intrigued.'

'Dylan and I have been discussing the situation and we'd like to help if we can, at least in the short term, while you're going through such a rough patch. So how would it be if we waived the rent on the workshop, with the proviso that we take a commission on all sales for the time-being, rather than just what we sell in the shop?'

Not for the first time, Faye and Dylan's generosity took her breath away. She was so fortunate to have such good friends.

She swallowed. 'That's a very generous offer, Faye, but I feel it's only fair to point out that Lyall has already offered to put some money into the business.'

'I know, he's told us. That needn't make any difference. We just want to see the business expanding, not disappearing like Jack. After all, from a purely selfish motive, we've got a vested interest, because we can sell your jewellery over and over again in our shop, as you well know.'

Something occurred to Katie, and she felt she had to voice her thoughts.

'So what if Jack decides to come back?'

There were startled looks all round the table. 'Jack's gone, Katie,' Dylan said gently, 'and the sooner you accept that fact and get on without him the better.'

Without telling them about the e-mail and letter she had received, she couldn't make them understand and, for the time being, she thought it would be more prudent to keep that piece of information to herself.

'All the same, just supposing he straightened himself out and did manage to return to pay off his debts. What then?'

'I'd assume you'd contact the police, if he had the gall to show up here. Katie, surely you wouldn't take him back?'

'Until he's had a chance to explain then I'm not prepared to judge him. I've known Jack for the best part of a year and, during that time, he's been a good friend and colleague, as I'm sure Shelley will testify.'

Faye could see that her friend was more upset than she had admitted at Jack's disappearance and, always the peacemaker, said soothingly, 'Well, we'll just have to see what transpires, but I wouldn't hold your breath, if I were you, love.'

There was a silence and then Dylan got up to fetch the coffee. They moved into the sitting-room and Lyall came to sit beside Katie on the sofa. She inched away from him, determined not to lose her head just because he had good looks.

They spent the rest of the evening talking about general issues concerned with the village and, presently, Katie got up to leave.

'I'll walk you home,' Lyall offered.

'There's no need,' she assured him

and intercepted a puzzled look from Faye.

'Oh, but there most certainly is. I wouldn't allow you to walk off in the dark when I live practically next door.'

Reluctantly she agreed, then thanked Faye and Dylan for a lovely meal and set off beside Lyall. The path was dimly lit and, as they crossed the narrow lane, he took hold of her arm and she felt as if his fingers were burning into her flesh.

Having seen her into the cottage, he muttered goodbye and disappeared into the darkness and she realised that she had enjoyed the evening more than she cared to admit.

The next morning, Katie decided to make an early start at the workshop. To her surprise, she found Lyall already there, hard at work. He looked up and grinned. 'Great minds think alike, eh? Coffee's on.'

For a time they worked in companionable silence. Her silver jewellery required a lot of concentration. At present, she was engrossed in chasing — putting a simple line decoration on a bracelet.

Lyall said, 'I'm going for a leg stretch. I won't be long and then we'll have coffee. By the way, where's Shelley this morning?'

Katie explained about Shelley supplementing her income by working in the local pub in the evenings and often having to do chores for her family before setting out in the morning. He left the workshop to return a few minutes later clutching a bulging carrier bag.

'Croissants. Dylan's heated them up for us. I only had a scratch breakfast and suspect you did, too. We could do with a microwave in here.'

Shelley put in an appearance just then and, over coffee and croissants, Lyall said, 'We really need to talk, guys, about this venture of ours. It's necessary to see if it's all going to come together, isn't it?'

'Oh, it'll all be all right on the night,' Katie assured him, sounding more confident than she felt.

'Hmm, but I still think we need a proper plan,' he insisted. 'What's your opinion on this, Shelley?'

Shelley seemed surprised that he had asked her. 'Me? Oh, I'm happy to leave the decision making to you and Katie. I just want to get on with making my jewellery.' And with this remark, she got up and went into the back room.

As Lyall came to stand beside her, Katie smelt the fresh fragrance of his cologne, a mixture of musky woodland scents, and she suddenly had an irresistible urge to reach out and touch him and wondered if he were aware of the magnetism too.

As if reading her thoughts, his hazel eyes met her topaz blue ones and he gave her a devastating smile. Just then Shelley returned and the moment was gone.

They spent the next twenty minutes discussing the layout for the exhibition. Katie had to admit that Lyall was so full of ideas that he fired them with enthusiasm and spurred them into action so that, by the end of the day, they had made great headway and things were certainly beginning to look up.

★ ★ ★

Katie was in the middle of supper when the phone rang. When she picked up the receiver there was silence.

'Who is this?' she asked irritated.

She was just about to slam it down when Jack's voice said, 'Katie, it's me. Are you alone?'

Relief flooded through her. 'Jack, thank goodness! What on earth's going on? And where are you?'

'In a call box. I haven't much change.'

'Then give me the number, I'll call you back.'

'No. It's best you don't know where I am. I'm in big trouble, Katie, and just needed to get away, but I didn't want to leave without saying I'm sorry for what's happened.'

'And so you should be! We trusted you, Jack and you stole from us, there's no other word for it! I just can't believe the way you've behaved. You'd better have a good explanation.'

'Please, Katie, one day I promise I'll repay you, just trust me.'

'I don't know if I can. You've let Shelley and I down very badly, Jack, disappearing like that with the exhibition such a short way away. Return everything and then we can talk.'

There was a silence and then he said, 'I only wish I could, Katie, but I'm afraid that's not possible. I don't have the things any more.'

She was exasperated. 'What d'you mean? What have you done with our exhibits and the money from our account?'

There was a pause and then he said, 'I was in debt, Katie.'

'So you robbed us in order to pay off your creditors!' She was incensed. 'I don't believe this! How could you, Jack?

Why didn't you confide in me?'

'You were on holiday,' he reminded her quietly.

She swallowed, aware that if she vented her anger on him he'd more than likely ring off and then she would lose contact with him altogether.

'If it hadn't been for Lyall Travis offering to help out, Shelley and I would have been finished,' she told him now.

'Lyall! What exactly did he tell you?' Jack sounded suddenly wary.

She told him what Lyall had said and how he had stepped in to help them with the exhibition.

When she had finished, Jack said, 'It was because of Lyall Travis that . . . ' Infuriatingly his voice died away as his money ran out and she was left staring at the receiver and wondering what on earth he had been about to say.

4

Later that evening, as Katie was doing some paperwork, the phone rang again, making her nearly jump out of her skin. To her relief, this time it was Aunt Alice. Katie was so pleased to hear her voice and suddenly everything seemed normal again.

'Mary's daughter's returned from holiday, and so she's able to take over from me now. There's really no longer any need for me to stay. I'm thinking of coming home in a few days' time.'

'I'm delighted to hear it. We've all missed you,' Katie told her old friend.

'How's Jack? I haven't heard a word from the young rascal since I've been away.'

'Oh, he's fine,' Katie said, hoping she would be forgiven for the white lie. 'He's away by himself for a few days, one or two things to sort out on the financial front, you know.'

Aunt Alice chuckled. 'Sounds like Jack — and Lyall Travis?'

'Oh, he's turned out to be a godsend. He's quite an artist, you know, so he's producing some pieces of jewellery for our exhibition.'

They chatted for a time and, much to her relief, no further questions were asked about Jack.

Katie had a restless night, mulling things over in her head and wondering if she should mention Jack's phone call to Lyall. In the end, however, she decided it would be best to wait and see if Jack contacted her again. If only he had finished what he had started to say about Lyall. She had an uneasy feeling that she wouldn't like what he had to tell her, but she really needed to know.

After all, supposing she had been misjudging him and the root of the problem had been Lyall all along. Per-haps he hadn't told her the truth about what had really happened between himself and Jack whilst she had been away. She eventually drifted off into a deep sleep to awaken unrefreshed, with a headache.

Lyall was already hard at work when she arrived at the workshop. 'Night on the tiles?' he wanted to know, surveying her pale face with interest.

'Certainly not, not that it's any of your business!' she snapped and he winked at her, hazel eyes sparkling with amusement. She realised that this man had the ability to both charm and infuriate her.

Collecting her work, she settled at the bench and was soon immersed in engraving a complicated design on a bracelet. Soon her ill humour evaporated with her headache.

After a short while, Shelley joined them and they worked in silence for the next half hour or so. Lyall set down the cuff links he had been working on and got to his feet.

'Faye tells me you would have been at a craft fair this weekend if Jack hadn't made off with your stuff.'

'Well, that was the original plan, but we've had to abandon it for this year,' Shelley told him. 'Just as well really because it's my youngest niece's birthday and I've promised to help her with her party. I'm an expert at blowing up balloons, don't you know!'

'Full of hot air, eh?' Lyall teased. 'So where exactly is this craft fair tomorrow?'

'Oh, near Tunbridge Wells,' Shelley informed him. 'The seasoned exhibitors do a kind of circuit round most of the craft fairs. It's a good way of making yourself known to the public. We'd just managed to get two or three slots and now we're going to have to miss this one.'

'Sounds as if Jack's got a lot to answer for. I suppose neither of you have heard from him?'

'Not a dicky bird,' Shelly told him, and Katie shook her head, unable to meet his eyes. Lying did not come naturally to her and, normally, she despised this kind of deception. When she finally looked up, she found Lyall studying her thoughtfully and was certain that he didn't believe her. Could it be that Jack had been in contact with him too?

Lyall consulted his watch. 'I've got to collect a few items from my friends in Sevenoaks this afternoon, but I'm sure the pair of you can manage perfectly well without me.'

Shortly after he had departed, Shelley announced that she had just remembered she'd got a dental appointment at two o'clock and so she went off too.

Left alone, Katie found it difficult to concentrate. After a while, she decided to call it a day and returned to the cottage.

Jack made no attempt to get in touch with her again that evening, and she realised that it would be ridiculous to hang about the entire time, on the off chance that he might ring. She was surprised that he hadn't at least tried to text her, but, perhaps, he thought it would be too risky to use her mobile phone number.

The next morning was glorious, June at its very best. She had a leisurely breakfast in the small cottage garden which, at this time of year, was a tangle of roses and honeysuckle. She had a small paved area with pots full of petunias and deep blue trailing lobelia.

She was back in the kitchen when there was a knock at the front door. Her first thoughts were of Jack, but it was Lyall standing on the doorstep clutching the milk. 'It's much too nice a day to be moping indoors . . . Let's go to the craft fair anyway.'

She gaped at him. 'Whatever for? We've absolutely nothing to sell and it's no good accepting orders we can't possibly fulfil.'

'Granted, but there's no harm in taking a look at the opposition, is there? After all, how often do you get the chance to wander around and see what's on show?'

She considered, head on one side, her beautiful topaz blue eyes suddenly sparkling. 'You could have a point.

Some of the other folk there will also be exhibiting in London, so it could be useful to see the competition and, of course, there are lots of other things to see besides the jewellery.'

He smiled at her sudden enthusiasm. 'Good. You'll come then?'

'You'll have to wait whilst I change.'

When she came downstairs a few minutes later, dressed in a smart black skirt and a pink top, it was to find Lyall doing the washing up. 'Oh, there's really no need . . . '

He grinned. 'There's every need. You'll only have it to face when you get back. Anyway, I helped myself to a cup of coffee. You're looking very stylish.'

'Thanks.' Feeling a warm glow at the compliment, she swept up her jacket and bag.

'Aren't you forgetting something?' He looked so amused that she felt the colour rise to her cheeks, as she wondered if her skirt was hitched up or something. Smilingly, he indicated her feet and she realised she was still

71

wearing her fluffy pink bedroom slippers.

Laughingly, she found her shoes, and a few moments later they were speeding away into the Kent countryside past fields of grazing sheep and hedgerows dotted with pale pink dog roses.

Once again she discovered him to be an easy companion, silent for a time and then chatting about general topics of interest. They stopped for coffee en route because, as Lyall said, on this occasion they weren't in any particular hurry.

They chatted over cups of cappuccino and she found herself relaxing in the pleasant atmosphere of the hotel lounge. It wasn't until she had told him about her art degree course and a fair amount about her family that, rather belatedly, she recognised the skilful manner in which he was getting her to talk about herself. Well, she didn't intend to tell him about Peter, not yet at any rate.

She buttered a second scone. 'All right, so you've managed to discover all this about me, but what about you?'

His hazel eyes flickered, as if she had caught him off guard, but he answered coolly enough. 'If you think I've got any skeletons in the cupboard then you'll be sadly disappointed. What in particular would you like to know about me?'

'Well, a bit about your background would be a good starting point.'

'OK, I was born in London but, when I was around ten, my father died and so we moved to Derbyshire to live with my grandparents. My mother married a couple of years later and my sister arrived about a year after that. She lives in Australia, but I've already told you that.'

And what about relationships? She wanted to ask him, still convinced that he had come to Lyndhurst to recover from a broken love affair, as she herself had done, but before she could ask him anything further, he looked at his watch and got to his feet.

'We'd best be making tracks if we're to get to this craft fair before lunchtime.

You can have the next fascinating instalment of my life history another time.'

It was interesting to wander round the craft fair. Usually, when Katie had been manning a stall she only took a break of half an hour or so, and spent most of that chatting with her friends. She knew several of the stall holders and they naturally wanted to know where Jack and Shelley were, and why they hadn't got a stall.

Lyall attracted a number of curious glances, but she was relieved that he was there to help her ward off difficult questions.

'So what do you reckon to the opposition?' he asked her now, as they moved away from a jewellery stand.

'Oh, that last lot of jewellery was very attractive, but not very original. I reckon we can do equally as well, given half a chance.'

'Of course, our goods are a bit pricey,' he ventured.

'I refuse to sell tat,' she snapped back

and, smilingly, he took her arm and steered her towards another stall.

'I wasn't criticising, just making a point. Our stuff is real class. It'll knock 'em dead.'

Relaxing she laughed. 'I'm not sure if that's my objective. Anyway, thanks for the vote of confidence!'

She was all too aware of his hand on her arm and an odd little frisson shuddered down her spine. The man at her side was undeniably attractive, but what exactly did she know about him? So far he had told her very little about himself, and she couldn't help feeling there was a great deal more to find out.

She tried to ignore the arm. 'There's a refreshment tent over there, behind that group of trees, but it'll probably be crowded.'

It was rather a crush and quite noisy in the tent, but surprisingly, they were serving good ploughman's lunches, which washed down with ice-cold lemonade shandy proved most acceptable. Katie spotted a couple of people she knew and waved to them. They came across bearing laden trays.

'What's this, taking a sabbatical?' the cheerful red-head asked, as her companion fetched a couple of chairs.

'Oh, I thought it would make a change to wander round and eye up the competition for once,' Katie said carefully.

The girl laughed. 'You've got nothing to worry about, has she, James?' She looked meaningfully at Lyall. 'Aren't you going to introduce us to your friend, Katie?'

'Lyall Travis, Rachel Saunders and James Humphries. Lyall's just joined our team in Lyndhurst. Actually, we've had to pull out from this function because we've got a bit behind with our work for the exhibition. Jack's the one who's taken the sabbatical, it seems he needed a break.'

Rachel raised her eyebrows. 'You're kidding, but we only saw him a week or so ago, and he never said a word.'

Katie frowned. 'Where was this, Rachel?'

'Oh, you know that exhibition in Croydon. I must admit I was a bit puzzled, as you'd said you definitely weren't going to be there. Actually, we'd got no intention of going ourselves, had we, James? But as we happened to be in Surrey, at the time, we decided to pop in. Jack said you and Shelley were taking an early lunch break — probably round the shops. What's wrong, Katie?'

The slightest pressure on her arm from Lyall made her say quickly, 'Nothing, nothing at all. I was just surprised that you'd been there, that's all. Jack forgot to mention it.'

Her mind was racing on. If Jack had gone to that particular exhibition then he must have been selling their stock. She couldn't question Rachel any more, but she was incensed to think how he had double-crossed them and how easily. He had made off with several hundred pounds worth of stock and raw materials and, for all she knew, probably intended to set up in business again and use their original designs to copy from.

Aunt Alice returned to Lyndhurst on Tuesday and Katie stopped by to see her during her lunch-break.

Alice Mason gave Katie a warm hug, her kindly face wreathed in smiles. As they sat exchanging news over a cup of tea, Katie thought how tired the older woman was looking. She pushed a letter towards Katie. 'This was waiting for me when I got back. It's from Jack. You should have told me! I suppose I oughtn't to be surprised that he's gone off into the blue, but I shall miss him. Go on read it, dear. At least he had the decency to write before he took off . . . posted it in London on his way to goodness knows where.'

It was brief and to the point.

Dear Aunt Alice,

I'm sorry to let you know like this, but something's cropped up and I've got to move on. These past months in Lyndhurst have been good, but now it's time for me to leave. Thanks for everything and please don't think too badly of me,

Jack.

P.S. I've taken the silver cigarette box. You told me Uncle George had left it to me anyway, so I didn't think you'd mind.

'If only he'd asked I'd have let him have it then and there,' Aunt Alice said, shaking her silvery head sadly, her blue eyes misting over. 'He's a young scallywag, but I'll miss him, sorely.' She reached out and took Katie's small hands between her own gnarled ones.

'And what about you, dear? I had such hopes for the pair of you.'

Katie looked at her in surprise. 'We made a good team, Aunt Alice, but if you mean what I think you do, then there was never anything more than friendship between us. I thought of Jack as a loveable, but sometimes irritating, younger brother. Anyway, this has certainly taught me one thing.'

'What's that, dear?'

'Never to trust a man, and I won't,

not ever again,' she vowed bitterly.

'Oh dear, that sounds very final. I suppose what with Peter and now Jack you must be feeling very let down.'

Katie nodded, remembering with sadness, how Peter had led her to believe they would be married just as soon as they had saved enough, and then had gone off on a conference up north and met a woman ten years his senior with a young child. Before Katie could get her head round it, he had left his job in Dorset and moved in with her.

Katie blinked, surprised at how vulnerable she still felt where Peter was concerned. She had moved to Lyndhurst to make a fresh start and because her grandmother needed her, but now Gran was gone, Jack had let her down, Lyall Travis had appeared on the scene, and life was getting complicated all over again.

'Katie?' Aunt Alice peered at her anxiously.

'Oh, sorry, Aunt Alice. It was just such a shock to find Jack had cleared off like that, and I realise it must have been for you, too. We didn't want to say anything until you returned home. Thought you'd got quite enough to deal with as it was.'

Aunt Alice shook her head. 'Strangely enough I'd been half expecting it, but don't judge all men to be the same, dear. I'll admit that I'd hoped that you and Jack might make a go of things because I'm fond of you both, but it's probably just as well you didn't, the way things have turned out.'

Katie smiled ruefully. 'I learnt a very salutary lesson where Peter was concerned, and I'm just not prepared to make that mistake again.'

But, even as Katie spoke these words, the image of a tall, fair-haired man with piercing hazel eyes and a devastating smile came unbidden into her mind and she knew that Lyall Travis had somehow managed to get under her skin.

Alice Mason poured more tea. 'Oh, you don't really mean that, dear. Yes, you've been hurt, but eventually time will heal and Mr Right will come along.'

She handed Katie her cup. 'Now tell me how you're getting on with Lyall Travis. Thank goodness he was around when all this happened!'

Katie had been wondering when the subject of Lyall would crop up. 'Now I'm glad you've mentioned him, Aunt Alice . . . just who exactly is he? I know he and his family came to stay with you when he was a child, but I suspect there's more to it than that. It was a bit of a shock to find he'd moved into the flat and taken charge of things whilst I was away, I can tell you.'

Aunt Alice looked positively taken aback. 'You mean he didn't explain?'

Katie shook her head and the old lady continued to look puzzled.

'Well then he must have assumed I had. I'm sure he'd have said, if you'd asked. He was very straightforward with me, which is what decided me to rent him the flat and, in the circumstances, it's just as well he was here to sort things out.'

In exasperation Katie prompted, 'So who is he then?'

'Why he's a friend of Jack's, of course.'

Katie was flabbergasted. She stared at Aunt Alice open-mouthed. Suddenly things began to slot into place, at least she thought they did.

Slowly she said, 'Some friend he's turned out to be. If he's caused him to disappear. What exactly did he have on Jack to make him run off like that?'

Alice Mason seemed startled by Katie's words. 'Oh, you mustn't blame Lyall, dear. I'm sure it wasn't his fault. We'll just have to wait and see what happens. Anyway, fond as I was of Jack, still am for that matter, I think it'll be for the best in the long run.'

'What will?' demanded Katie.

Aunt Alice reached for the sugar. 'That he's gone, of course. After all, I hardly thought he'd stay for ever . . . a pity though. If only things could have worked out differently, but it wasn't to be.'

Katie was tempted to ask her, 'What

things?' and 'What wasn't to be?' but thought better of it. Inwardly, she was seething. Just wait until she saw Lyall!

After extracting a shopping list from Aunt Alice for the following day and stooping to stroke Sheba, she went out into the sunshine.

A few minutes later, Katie stormed into the workshop to find only Shelley at the bench. 'Where's Lyall?' she practically shouted at her.

'He's gone over to Sevenoaks. Says he can't do anything further until tomorrow morning. Whatever's wrong, Katie?'

'Shelley, did you know that Lyall and Jack were so-called friends?'

Shelley shifted uncomfortably and lowered her eyes beneath Katie's searching gaze.

'You did, didn't you? Why on earth didn't you tell me?'

Shelley, who had never seen Katie so angry before, remained silent.

'Come on, Shelley. It was because Lyall told you not to, wasn't it?'

Shelley nodded. 'Sorry, Katie. What was it he said now?' She screwed up her pretty face in concentration. 'I know, that you'd mis-misconstrue the situation because you'd been away when he arrived and you'd think he'd had something to do with Jack going off like that.'

'Too right! If you ask me, Lyall's the conman, not Jack. Just wait until I catch up with him. He's got an awful lot of explaining to do. He's certainly taken me for a ride!'

Shelley looked worried. 'Lyall's a nice guy, Katie. I'm sure he wouldn't have done anything to make Jack go off like that. He's done everything in his power to help us, after all.'

'And you're a nice trusting girl, Shelley, but if he can deceive me over one thing then he can deceive me over another.'

5

On Wednesday, Katie usually went into the next village to do some shopping. She finally caught up with Lyall in the local mini market.

'Just dong a bit of shopping for Mrs Mason,' he said by way of a greeting.

Surprised at suddenly meeting up with him like this, she said inanely, 'Snap, so am I, ought we to compare shopping lists?'

He laughed. 'Hardly, Mrs Mason's offered to cook my supper tonight so I said I'd get the ingredients. You look as if you've bought the basics. She obviously didn't want to hurt either of our feelings. Nice she's back, eh?'

'It certainly is. So why did you go off yesterday afternoon just when she'd returned?'

'I naturally assumed you'd want to

spend a bit of time with Aunt Alice on your own.'

'Mrs Mason to you,' she flared and his eyes flickered with amusement.

'As a matter of fact, I took my friend's niece out to dinner. She's just returned to England after backpacking round Australia. Such an interesting girl.'

Katie told herself that she couldn't have cared less what he did in his private life, but, deep down, knew that this wasn't true and was annoyed with herself for even registering this fact.

Murmuring something about tea-bags, she marched off down the aisle.

A few minutes later, having got through the check-out in record time, she swept up her carriers and went off to stow them in the boot of her car. She had a strong feeling that Aunt Alice had contrived to send them both shopping at the same time so that they would inevitably meet up.

Lyall came across to her from the opposite end of the car park. 'OK, I'll admit it was hardly a coincidence, us bumping into each other like this. Mrs Mason told me where to find you. Said this was your usual routine midweek, and that you were out for my blood. I always believe in getting matters out in the open, so let's discuss what's bothering you in a civilised manner over coffee, shall we?'

She glared at him. 'You know perfectly well what's wrong,' she said angrily, 'If you care to examine your conscience!'

'Coffee,' he said and marched off in the direction of the nearby café.

Katie, followed him reluctantly, irritated by the way he had taken command of the situation. She was an independent girl and didn't want to be manipulated. He assumed she would join him for coffee and some perverse part of her made her want to refuse, but she knew things needed sorting out once and for all. She stored all her grievances up, waiting to fire them at him at the first opportunity.

The village café was excellent and the coffee and home-made biscuits helped to restore her to her usual calm self.

'Well, go on then, I can see you bursting to say something,' he said.

'Too right I am. Why didn't you tell me you and Jack were friends?'

He sipped his coffee. 'Didn't I?'

'You know perfectly well, you didn't. All this time I've been wondering why Jack took off like that. Well, it's pretty obvious, isn't it?'

'Tell me.' He leant back in his chair, hazel eyes narrowed, watching her with interest so that she felt uncomfortably aware that she was the one being interrogated.

'You found out that Jack was living here and came to see him. The pair of you had a disagreement, probably about something that had happened between you in the past.

You put pressure on him and he felt he couldn't cope so he went off. Why on earth couldn't you have left him alone? Everything was going so well

89

until you appeared on the scene!'

He shook his head, knowing that he was going to have his work cut out to convince her of what he was about to say. 'Are you quite sure about that? I think you'll find that Jack would have gone off regardless of whether I'd turned up or not. Let's say that I might have hastened his departure, but only fractionally. The chances are he would have disappeared into the sunset at any time anyway, because he's a bit of a rolling stone.

'Yes, I suppose you could say we were friends, at one time at any rate, but he let me down badly. Seems to be making a habit of it. He's very unreliable, Katie, always has been, although I thought perhaps he'd changed. He seemed happy enough in Lyndhurst, more mature somehow, but, unfortunately, a leopard doesn't change its spots.'

Katie remembered that when Jack had 'phoned her, he'd said he was in trouble. She felt an odd prickle at the back of her neck. Could Lyall have some kind of hold on him?

'Were you blackmailing him?' she asked in a whisper.

His expression of utter incredulity told her how wide of the mark she was. He gave a harsh laugh. 'Don't be ridiculous! You obviously doubt my integrity, but were perfectly happy to trust Jack.'

Katie glared at him. 'Jack is Aunt Alice's nephew. I don't know what you're implying, but you're obviously determined to blacken his character. Aunt Alice is very fond of Jack and, just because he's decided to move on, doesn't alter that. I'm sure there's a simple explanation for his behaviour and suspect you could shed some light on the matter if you'd a mind to do so.'

He shrugged. 'Have it your own way.'

She suddenly saw red. 'What exactly is it between the two of you?'

His mouth was set in a grim line. 'You'll have to ask Jack that question. If you ever manage to catch up with him, of course. Anyway, it was his choice to leave Lyndhurst. I didn't force him to, contrary to what you might believe.'

They sat in silence for a few minutes and then he said, 'We have to accept that Jack's gone walk-about for reasons best known to himself, and it's pretty obvious he's not coming back. I realise you're continuing to find it difficult to trust me, and perhaps in your shoes I'd feel the same. Anyway, at the end of the day, it's up to you and, if you'd rather not have my input then just say the word and I'll move on as well.'

This speech took Katie completely by surprise. She supposed she had been rather ungracious and deserved this.

She took a deep breath. 'Perhaps I over-reacted. It was a bit of a shock, that's all, but Shelley and I wouldn't want you to pull out. Actually, we don't have much option do we?' she added honestly.

Lyall laughed. 'Well, you have the decency to admit that, at least. I'll tell you what, I'll help you out of this mess and then we'll discuss things further, but we'll need to call a truce. We'll never get anywhere if we're always at loggerheads.'

He extended his hand and she took it reluctantly, but then was startled by the sudden intensity of feelings that flooded through her. Her eyes locked with his and she wondered if he were aware of the chemistry too.

Releasing her hand abruptly, he got to his feet and the moment was over. 'Must press on, I'm afraid, or Mrs Mason will never get her shopping. See you later.'

With an effort, Katie pulled herself together. Lyall Travis might be good-looking and a charmer, but she had absolutely no intention of falling for him, besides he was obviously unavailable.

*　*　*

After a busy afternoon in the workshop, she spent the evening in the company of Dylan and Faye, relaxing over glasses of wine and showing them her holiday photographs, whilst endeavouring to put Lyall Travis out of her mind.

'Don't forget the quiz night on Friday,' Faye reminded her as she prepared to leave. 'Our team's depending on you, Katie!'

Katie gave her friend a thumbs up sign. 'I'll be there,' she promised. 'We'll beat them hollow!'

The quiz night in the village hall was in aid of the church roof fund. To Katie's astonishment, Lyall was there with Aunt Alice, an elderly neighbour and a tall, elegantly-dressed, willowy girl who smiled at Lyall enchantingly. He was an absolute caution, but her eyes kept straying in Lyall's direction and she wondered if the girl had been his dinner date on Tuesday night.

It was an enjoyable evening, and although some of the questions were taxing, Faye's team managed to pull into third place with Lyall's the outright winners, and the vicar and his family coming into second place.

As they queued for refreshments, she

was suddenly aware of Lyall standing beside her with the willowy girl.

'Olivia, this is Katherine Mead who runs the workshop I was telling you about. Olivia has just returned from the other side of the world.'

A pair of cold green eyes surveyed her. Olivia was an amazingly attractive girl with a cap of shiny dark hair and a flawless complexion, but Katie immediately summed her up as being a spoilt little rich girl, and then reprimanded herself for being so judgemental.

The hand that took hers was limp, and the girl said coolly, 'I simply had to come over to see where Lyall was staying. Lyndhurst's such a quaint place, isn't it? Quite why he insisted on coming to this event, I wouldn't know, but it's so typical of him, he's got such a charitable nature.'

Lyall was collecting cups of coffee from the opposite end of the hatch and Olivia added quietly. 'Don't underestimate him, will you, Katherine. He may have a kind heart, but he's not a soft option, you know.'

Katie met her gaze levelly, wondering what message the other girl was trying to convey. 'Oh, I'm fully aware of that. I can't imagine Lyall doing anything he didn't want to.'

Olivia smiled. 'Well, we go back a very long way. We met up again in Australia recently, and as soon as I returned to England he came to look me up.'

Katie had an inspiration. 'Do you also happen to know Lyall's friend, Jack Mason, Alice Mason's nephew?' she asked casually, watching for the other girl's reaction.

She frowned, 'I don't remember a Jack, but I've met a number of Lyall's friends. He's extremely popular, you know. I'm so pleased he's decided to stay here. It'll be such fun having him around.'

The queue had moved on leaving the two of them chatting.

'So what exactly do you do, Olivia?'

She arched her eyebrows. 'Oh, didn't

Lyall tell you? I'm in the fashion business. A buyer for a London store. It's easy to commute from Sevenoaks, but I've got my own flat up in town, so very convenient. I don't have to work, but I prefer to do my own thing, rather than being dependent on my family.'

Katie was relieved when, just then, Faye extricated herself from the president of the W.I. and made her way towards them. Olivia excused herself after a minute or two and went back to her table and Lyall.

'Fraternising with the opposition?' Faye enquired as they collected their refreshments.

'Trying to find out if she knows Jack, but if she does she's not admitting it.'

Faye did a balancing act with several plates of sandwiches. 'If you want my advice, Luv, I'd put Jack out of your mind and concentrate on that exhibition. Life's got to go on.'

Dylan, obviously getting hungry, signalled to them just then and they hurried back to their table. Turning her head, Katie caught a glimpse of Lyall and Olivia, whose arm was linked through his, as they spoke with the vicar and his wife. Katie felt a slight pang of envy, as she noticed the ease of the relationship and the way they laughed at some shared joke together.

★　★　★

By the time Lyall arrived on Monday morning, Katie and Shelley were already hard at work. 'I thought the Wine and Wisdom was a good evening,' he remarked, settling himself at the work-bench. 'Olivia enjoyed it immensely.'

Katie didn't look up. 'You surprise me. I thought she considered it to be rather parochial.'

Shelley got up to make some coffee and he said, sotto voice. 'Mrs Mason found a message on the answer 'phone from Jack last night. He must have left it while she was at church.'

Katie felt her heartbeat quicken. 'Where is he? What's happened?'

'I've no idea where he was calling from, he used his mobile. Mrs Mason reckons he sounded very remorseful. Said he was sorry for all the trouble he'd caused and that he'd like to see her before he finally moved on, but didn't know if that would be possible.'

'I wish he'd just go, and then perhaps we could all get on with our lives,' she said vehemently.

Lyall shot her a puzzled look. 'Do I take it he'd been in touch with you, too?'

She swallowed, realising there was no point in denying it now.

'Yes, as a matter of fact he has, but not recently. Anyway, it really doesn't matter because, from today, I'm making a fresh start and putting him out of my mind.'

He gave a slight smile. 'I'm glad to hear it. You've got to move on.'

Katie examined the necklace she had just completed. 'Was Aunt Alice upset?'

'Well naturally a little, but older people sometimes seem more able to accept things as inevitable. I think she found Jack rather a restless individual. He turned up out of the blue and now he's vanished back into it again.'

She gave him a searching glance. 'And I suppose that's exactly what you'll do in a few weeks' time.'

His expression was impassive. 'I'm not sure I follow you.'

'Mosey off into the sunset, back from where you came from.'

'And is that what you'd like me to do, Katherine Mead?'

She considered, head on one side, blue eyes serious. 'I'm not sure yet. If it's going to mean letting us down all over again then I'd rather get it over and done with, but if you're serious about us and our venture and really want to stay in Lyndhurst then, obviously, that would put a different complexion on things.'

He set down the cuff links he was working on, sensing that Katie desperately needed his reassurance.

'So all it takes now is for you to begin to trust me, Katherine Mead and then we can take if from there.'

Before she could reply, Shelley came back into the room with the coffee.

'Time for a pow wow,' Lyall said taking the tray from her. 'This exhibition is looming ever nearer and the time scale is bothering me. It seems we need a bit of strategy if we're going to be ready on time.'

Shelley, who looked as if she hadn't got the remotest idea of what he was talking about, munched on a chocolate digestive and nodded in agreement. She was an affable girl and organisation was not her strongest point.

'Now wait a minute! Shelley, don't just sit there and let Lyall make all the decisions. What do you think?'

Shelley gazed into her coffee, as if for inspiration. 'Oh, you know me, I'm happy to go with the flow.'

'Huh!' Katie's body language said it all. 'I would remind you that there are three of us involved in this project.

Right from the outset, I told you we'd got some drawings for the layout, Lyall.'

He sighed impatiently. Aware that he was treading on eggshells, but determined to put his point across. 'And, right from the outset, I told you that, until I'd had an opportunity to think things through, I wasn't interested in seeing them. Now I have and I am, so can I take a look, please?'

She extracted the drawings from her portfolio in silence, and he studied them carefully, before producing some of his own and putting them beside them. Eventually, he selected a couple from the pile Katie had given him and put two of his own with them. Finally, he held up the drawings he'd chosen for their inspection.

'As you can see, there's a certain similarity of thought. We're not so very far apart in our ideas.'

'That's because those two drawings are Jack's,' Katie told him stonily. 'Mine are the ones that you've pushed to the bottom of the pile!'

Shelley gave a little laugh, caught Katie's gaze and busied herself with her work again.

Lyall set Jack's ideas aside and considered Katie's instead. 'OK, if we put this one of yours, and say this one of mine together, then I would think it might just work, although there's still something not quite right . . . '

'Hang on!' Shelley sprang to her feet and went round to his side. 'I've got it! This is what's missing!' She grabbed a piece of paper and, with a few swift strokes, pencilled in one or two extra details.

'That's a stroke of genius, Shelley! Why didn't I think of that?' Lyall asked, head on one side, and Katie had to agree. Shelley, for all her reluctance to participate in a brainstorming session, had triumphantly come up with the solution and saved the day.

'Layout is extremely important,' Lyall reminded them. 'An eyecatching display is going to attract the judges. Now we must concentrate on the centrepiece, something stunning to connect all three themes, but not the obvious flower arrangement. Any thoughts on the matter?'

The two girls shook their heads and, after a couple of hours hard work, during which they spoke very little Lyall said, 'I fancy a bite of lunch, my treat. How about Faye and Dylan's place?'

'They're closed today,' Katie told him.

'Right. Then how about our local hostelry?'

Shelley groaned. 'I see enough of it in the evenings when I'm working behind the bar. Thanks, but no thanks. I'll tell you what, Lyall, I'll take a raincheck, if you don't mind. I could do with finishing a bit earlier today.'

He nodded and looked across at Katie, who hesitated only fractionally before saying, 'Actually, I'm starving. I only had a sketchy breakfast.' It was, she decided, time to bury the hatchet! 'D'you want anything from the baker's, Shelley?'

But Shelley, absorbed in her enamelling once more, reached for another chocolate biscuit and shook her head.

In the end, Lyall took Katie to The Malt Shovel in the next village, where they did good bar snacks and there were alcoves for them to sit comfortably without being jostled by elbows, as in the pub in Lyndhurst. Katie realised how hungry she was and tucked into scampi and chips washed down by lager.

'There are a few things we need to iron out, now we're out of Shelley's earshot,' Lyall said.

Katie looked at him in surprise. 'Oh, but I thought you valued her input.'

'Where work is concerned of course I do, and it would be most unjust to leave her out of any discussion. No, Katie, I'm talking about our own working relationship.'

'What exactly are you getting at, Lyall?'

His hazel eyes swept her face and the slightly long fair hair fell forward over his forehead, making him look boyish. He sighed. 'You don't make it easy for me, Katie. I'd like us to get on for Alice Mason's sake, but you still seem to resent me. I know I can't take Jack's place, but we ought to, at least, make an effort to get on whilst we're working.'

Her eyes smouldered. 'The workshop was my enterprise originally. It's a project close to my heart. I put most of the capital into it. Money given me by my grandmother, and the others contributed towards the rent. We split any profits. Jack and Shelley were happy to leave most of the decision making to me, and everything was going well, but now you've come along and seem to think you can take over.

'It must be wonderful to be so sure of yourself. Well, I for one am not taken in by your charm, even if the rest of the population of Lyndhurst are. What makes you think you've got the right to tell us what to do?'

There, she had said it now. Lyall looked positively amazed by this onslaught, and for a moment or two there was a strained silence, and then he set down his knife and fork and said icily, 'We've been through this all before, Katie, and I thought we'd sorted it out.

'Well, even at this late stage I'll opt out, if you prefer it that way. After all, there must be plenty of others who'd be more than happy to join forces with you, but you can kiss goodbye to this particular exhibition that you seem to have set your heart on so much!'

He had called her bluff and she knew she deserved it, for she was behaving in a ridiculously childish behaviour. She swallowed hard. 'No, Lyall, it's OK. I know I've given you a rough ride and there's no real excuse. It's just that you seem to want to be in control and I've been used to managing things myself. On the whole, it all seemed to be going quite well, even if I have made a bit of a hash of things at times.'

His expression softened. 'You think I've been a bit high-handed coming in and taking over like that? Well, maybe you've got a point.'

Katie made a pattern with the peas on her plate. 'You've made it painfully clear that you could do things a whole lot better, so the easy option would be for Shelley and I to sit back and let you take charge. However, I happen to think that we were making a reasonable job of things before you arrived on the scene. OK, so perhaps we could improve on our marketing strategies, and I'm prepared to accept your expertise in that direction, providing you realise that we can't take on orders we aren't able to fulfil until after the exhibition.

'I'm not setting out to become a millionairess, just to earn enough to keep me independent, and I happen to enjoy what I'm doing, and that goes for Shelley too.'

Surprisingly enough, he inclined his head and said, 'I know, and I don't want to change any of that. After all, I can't give you any idea of how long I'll be around before I become interested in some other project.'

He grinned suddenly. 'Now before you give me my marching orders, for the umpteenth time, how would it be if I promise to handle things differently in future rather than just charging in like a bull in a china shop.'

She was forced to smile. 'I know I can be a bit stubborn. You see, when things are going along OK, I honestly can't see the point in change for change's sake, and Shelley, bless her, has always been happy to leave the management side to myself.'

'Well, from now on we'll be more up front with one another, shall we? I'm aware that you're not too keen on my drifting off without telling you where I'm going, not that it's any of your business, of course.'

She glared at him. 'On that score you're just like Jack. He used to skive off for a session at the gym or an extended lunch break, but at least he'd say when he expected to be back.'

'Point taken. You know we'll have to have more business lunches like today.'

A few minutes later they left The Malt Shovel and, as Lyall said he needed some stamps, walked the short distance to the post office. Katie paused to look in the window of the antique shop and something immediately caught her attention.

'Lyall, come and look at this!'

He was by her side in an instant.

'What's wrong, Katie?'

She pointed to the centre of the display. 'Lyall, that's Aunt Alice's cigarette box, the one that Jack took!'

He whistled. 'It certainly looks like it, but are you sure?'

'Of course, I'd know it anywhere. Anyway, it's easy enough to identify. It's got a distinctive mark on the inside. I really can't believe Jack would stoop so low as to have sold it.'

'I could tell the owner it's stolen property.'

Katie shook her head. 'It would mean involving the police and we've already decided against that. I wonder how much they're asking for it?'

'Wait here, I'll go and ask. I might be able to make a few subtle enquiries as to how he came by it and, if it means so much to Aunt Alice, then I'd be only too pleased to redeem it.'

'Actually, it means a lot to me as well, Lyall.'

He stared at her. 'You see it was actually my grandparents who gave it to Aunt Alice and Uncle George for a silver wedding present, so it's of sentimental value. Oh, it's true, Aunt Alice did say Jack could have it, but she wouldn't have expected him to have sold it.'

6

A few minutes later, Lyall came out of the antique shop clutching a package and looking pleased with himself. 'I had a bit of a chat with the owner, did a deal, and he let me have it for a special price. He wasn't prepared to tell me how he came by it, though.'

'Thanks, Lyall, it'll make Aunt Alice's day, to say nothing of mine!'

He grinned. 'Then it was a worthwhile investment!'

As he drove the short distance back to Lyndhurst, Katie said, 'This trouble that Jack's in, do you happen to know what it might be, Lyall?'

He didn't reply for so long that she thought he hadn't heard her question, but as they approached the village, he broke the silence. 'Jack did something rather foolish which he now regrets, and only he can put it right. I thought he'd decided to remain in Lyndhurst, face the music, but he chose to leave and since then I haven't heard from him. I can only assume he's got himself into more trouble. He has been known to mix with some rather dubious types.'

Katie stared at him. 'You mean these so-called friends might have caught up with him, put pressure on him?'

Lyall shook his head. 'I honestly don't know, but I would advise you not to get involved. It's up to Jack to decide whether to come clean about what's happened, or make a fresh start for himself as far away from here as possible.'

'Then why doesn't he go? What exactly is there to keep him here?'

Lyall shrugged. 'Who can say? He's never been good at commitment, but he obviously enjoyed working at his pottery. Perhaps he's hoping for a second chance.'

Aunt Alice was thrilled by the return of the cigarette box and even shed a tear. She hugged Lyall. 'Thank you so much! Oh, I know what I said about not minding, but I'm afraid I was just trying to put on a brave front. I'm deeply hurt at the way Jack's behaved and would like to give him a piece of my mind. And you, young man, let's hope you don't do a vanishing act, too.'

Lyall perched on the sofa. 'Oh, I've got no intention of disappearing and, when and if I do decide to move on, I'll be sure to give you plenty of warning and come back to visit. You can't get rid of me that easily, and now I suppose Katie and I had better get back to the workshop or Shelley will think we've both cleared off!'

The minute they entered the workshop, Shelley informed Lyall, 'Your lady friend was on the phone just now. Said to ring her right back. Olive — no, that can't be right.'

'Olivia. Thanks.' He didn't correct her on the first score, Katie noted, so maybe that's how it was. She felt he could do better than Olivia.

'She said she couldn't reach you on

your mobile,' Shelley added as an afterthought.

'No, that would be right because I left it here, switched off!'

He went into the back room and, after a few minutes, returned looking slightly irritated, but was pleasant enough to both of them.

The pile of exhibition work was growing daily and Katie knew that the standard was good. The replacement items were, if anything, even better than the originals and Lyall's contribution was going to prove a great asset. Suddenly, Katie had every hope that things could soon start looking up for them and that there might be a life after Jack, after all.

She put the finishing touches to a silver bracelet and got up for a leg stretch. Lyall stood up at the same time.

'Sorry, guys, I've got to go. See you both tomorrow morning.'

'I guess he's gone to see the delectable Olive,' Shelley said when he was out of earshot.

'Olivia,' Katie corrected her automatically. 'Well, he's entitled to a life outside work, but she obviously only has to raise her little finger for him to come running.'

Shelley looked at her friend thoughtfully. 'Lucky old Olive! Anyway, did you have a nice lunch?'

'Yes, it was very pleasant. You should have come.' Katie filled Shelley in, but neglected to tell her about the cigarette box.

Shelley tidied her area. 'Actually, I like working with Lyall. He's more organised than Jack, but there is a sort of similarity, don't you think?'

Katie considered. 'In their work, do you mean? Otherwise I don't think they've got much in common.'

'Yes, of course I mean their work. They have a similar sort of style, even though Lyall is working on smaller items than Jack. Have you seen his latest batch of pendants just removed from the kiln?'

The ceramic necklaces were exquisitely executed. The designs were as bold as Jack's, but the colours were more subtle, pale greens and blues and lilacs, whereas Jack would have chosen bright yellows, reds and purples.

As Katie studied them, she could see what Shelley was getting at, although it hadn't occurred to her before. It was as if they had both studied under the same teacher.

'I can see what you mean regarding the ceramics, but if you take a look at Lyall's graphics, then there's really no resemblance. Perhaps he took a look at Jack's pottery, the few pieces he left behind, and thought he'd try to fit in with what he'd been doing. I have to say I actually prefer Lyall's work. It's not so garish and I think it will appeal to a more sophisticated taste.'

'I know where you're coming from, but I actually liked those bright colours of Jack's. It was right for younger people. Anyway, I suppose we'll just have to see what happens.'

'Yes, we'll need to find out how much interest the exhibition generates before we can make any decisions about the way forward. Time will tell, no doubt.'

Shelley consulted her watch. 'And it's time I was going, or I'll be late for my shift at the pub again. See you, Katie.'

Katie was invariably the last to finish because she could not hurry her silver work. Eventually, she packed her things away and locked up carefully. When she arrived back at the cottage, she found another message from Jack on the answer phone. It gave her quite a start to hear his voice after what had transpired that afternoon.

'I'm keeping a low profile, Katie. Don't worry about me, there are things I've got to sort out. I'll be in touch again soon.'

* * *

Katie couldn't seem to settle to anything after that. There was nothing on TV or in the newspaper to capture her interest. She prowled around the house like a caged animal and, in the end, decided to have an early night. She had just switched the kettle on to make herself a hot drink when there was a loud knock at the door. Cautiously, she put on the chain and Lyall's voice called out urgently.

'It's Lyall — open up, Katie, I need to speak to you.'

She unlocked the door and he almost shot inside. 'What on earth's the matter?' she demanded. 'Is it Aunt Alice?'

'No, but because I don't wish to alarm her, I came here first. I surprised some intruders at the workshop just now. The alarm was going off ninety to the dozen when I got there.'

She stared at him, her heart in her mouth. 'Had they got in?'

'Yes, through that side window that's a bit iffy. Anyway, I obviously gave them such a fright that they scarpered.'

She suddenly noticed he'd cut his hand. 'What have you done to your hand? Surely you didn't hit anyone?'

He looked down at his hand in surprise, as if unaware that he had hurt it. 'No, I was doing battle with the sash and must have grazed it.'

'Did they get anything?'

'Nothing of any significance. I had a quick look round, but I thought I'd better get you to come and check things out, and find out if you want to phone the police.'

'Did you get a good look at them?'

'No. They didn't hang around long enough for that. Just a group of youngsters, I reckon. I've probably disturbed any fingerprints. Actually, I think they were after Jack. I heard his name mentioned and shouted after them that he didn't live here any more.'

She shivered and he put an arm lightly about her shoulders. 'It's up to you what you want to do, Katie.'

In the end, they decided to call the police and, after dressing Lyall's hand, they went to take a look at the workshop together. Fortunately, the intruders hadn't time to do much damage, what with the alarm going off and Lyall startling them, but apparently they had stuffed their pockets with whatever they could find. Mainly Lyall's pendants and few tools, and had sprayed a rather rude message on one wall, together with some indecipherable hieroglyphics.

Fortunately, the police weren't too long in coming and, after taking a few details, had a quick look round and advised them to get some stronger window locks. As they departed they said they'd be back in the morning and not to touch anything.

Katie had a restless night remembering the phone message from Jack and wishing she had mentioned it to Lyall.

It was late morning by the time the police had finished at the workshop. Lyall rang to let Katie and Shelley know that they could go in and they arrived together.

'There's been a fresh development,' Lyall told them. 'Amazingly, the police apprehended the youths last night in Hastings. They were in a stolen car with a distinctive, personalised number plate.'

Katie felt an enormous surge of relief. 'But I don't understand. How did they connect them with the break-in?'

'They had the pendants,' Lyall said. 'I've given a statement to the police, managing to keep Jack's name out of it, and rung the glazier and the locksmith.'

They were in the midst of setting the place to rights when Olivia Finch turned up, dressed as if she were going to a garden party.

'So this is where it all happens. Really, Lyall, you're so difficult to get hold of, I thought it easier to drive over. After all, you did invite me to take a look round.'

Lyall took her arm and, after introducing her to Shelley, told her, 'I'm afraid this morning isn't exactly the best time you could have chosen, Livvy. As you can see, we've had a bit of a problem here, and we're only just getting straight again.' He explained in a few words what had happened and she frowned.

'How dreadful for you. Well, it's obviously no use hanging about here, so why don't you finish off what you're doing and take me out to lunch, darling?'

He smiled, but Katie could see from his expression that he was barely containing his impatience. 'Your timing is really rather unfortunate, Olivia. We're waiting for someone to fix the window and then I've got to work solidly to replace some of my pendants that were taken last night because, although the police have managed to retrieve most of them, they still need to hang on to them for a bit.'

Olivia pouted. 'Lyall, you really are the limit! I'm sorry you've had the break-in, but I would have thought you could have torn yourself away for a couple of hours to show me around the village.'

'Look, when I've finished this, we'll

have a coffee and then you can take a look round the village and come back a bit later when we've had a chance to tidy up.'

She reluctantly consented and wandered idly about the room, a bored expression on her face, picking up items from the workbench.

'Choose a pendant or some earrings,' Lyall offered as she examined a selection of his handicraft.

'Thanks, but to be perfectly honest, Lyall, it's not really my kind of thing,' she told him candidly.

He gave her a wry smile. 'Thank you for your vote of confidence. Perhaps you'd prefer something made by Shelley or Katie. Choose and I'll pay for it.'

She rejected, almost immediately, the display of enamelled work which was Shelley's offering and picked up a pair of earrings that Katie had recently finished, fashioned in the shape of an edelweiss, but put them down again saying,

'Actually, I prefer gold — more

sophisticated, don't you think?

Olivia was obviously set on being critical. 'I don't know how you can work in a place like this, Lyall. It's little more than an outhouse.'

'That's what makes it so ideal for our purpose.' He leaned the broom against the wall. 'Come on, I'll show you around this place now.'

'I can't find any biscuits,' Shelley announced, as she returned with the coffee, a few minutes later. 'Where have they gone?'

'I suppose we must have eaten them.'

Shelley giggled. 'No, Lyall and Olive Oyle.'

Katie indicated the room that housed the kiln and Shelley shrugged and set the coffee on the table. A few minutes later they reappeared, Olivia laughing at some remark he had made. She chose to ignore the others and, taking her coffee, went to sit by Lyall.

'So, when are we going to see that new play in London? Oh, don't say you've forgotten — Lyall, you are the limit! You promised to take me.'

'And so I shall but, at present, I'm just a tad busy. Now, are you staying for lunch? If so, you can nip down to the baker's and get us all some sandwiches.'

Olivia wrinkled her pert little nose delicately. 'Oh, I think if you're this busy I'd better leave you to it. There are a few things I need in Canterbury so I'll go over there this afternoon.'

He followed her out into the courtyard and was gone a while.

Shelley raised her eyebrows and looked pointedly in the direction of the door. 'What is she like? Spoilt little rich girl! Obviously, our company isn't good enough for Miss High and Mighty.'

Katie shared the same opinion and wondered whatever Lyall saw in the girl. Her one consolation was that he hadn't given in and taken her out to lunch.

At that point, Lyall returned, settled himself at the bench and remarked, 'Poor Olivia, she's at a bit of a loose end since returning from her trip Down Under.'

'I thought she had a job up in town,' Katie commented.

'So she has, but it's only part-time. Anyway, she's cheered up now I've arranged to take her out to dinner this evening.'

'Lucky Olivia,' Shelley said, echoing Katie's thoughts. 'I'll get some sarnies, shall I, for those of us that are still slumming it in here? Cheese and pickle do you?'

Katie hid a smile and didn't dare meet Shelley's eyes.

Lyall produced another batch of necklaces in record time and then glazed the cufflinks that had been locked out of harm's way in the kiln room. He was a distinct asset, working more swiftly than Jack and producing work of a more impressive standard, in Katie's opinion.

Jack's pottery had been undeniably good, but he had always approached his work in a rather laid back fashion and was exceptionally untidy, frequently leaving both Shelley and herself to clear up after him on many occasions. Lyall was quite the reverse — meticulous and often lending them a hand when he had finished tidying up his own area of the workshop.

He had transformed the kiln room, which had formerly been mainly Jack's domain and usually in an indescribable mess. If only things weren't so complicated, Katie felt she could have relaxed and enjoyed Lyall's company. Not that he was the slightest bit interested in her, particularly now that Olivia Finch had appeared on the scene.

Shelley had beavered away at her enamelling and Katie went across to admire the end results from a previous day's work. She had chosen bright cobalt blues, turquoises, reds and golds. The patterns were beautifully and intricately executed and extremely eye-catching.

'You've made such a marvellous contribution, Shelley. I don't know what we'd do without you, really I don't!'

Shelley beamed. 'D'you really think so? It's all I ever wanted to do, be creative.'

It was all she had wanted to do, too, Katie reflected as she made her way back to the cottage. She had thought she had it made when she moved back to Dorset after university. For a couple of years she had been blissfully happy, working and going out with Peter, but then he'd met Chloe and then, suddenly, it had all been over.

Now, just when she was getting her life back on track, Lyall had appeared on the scene and stirred up emotions she had convinced herself no longer existed.

★   ★   ★

It was Aunt Alice's birthday that Saturday. She was going to visit friends on Sunday for lunch, but hadn't planned to do anything on the actual day itself. On Friday, Lyall asked if Katie would like to join them on an outing the next day.

'Nothing too taxing, a nice country drive, stopping off for lunch somewhere. Any suggestions?'

'How about Rochester, if it isn't too far? Aunt Alice loves looking at antique shops and then there's the cathedral.'

Saturday was a bright sunny day full of promise. Katie dressed with more care than usual in a new pink silk dress which she had purchased in a rash moment. She brushed her hair until it shone, catching it back in a scarf.

They arrived in Rochester in time for coffee. Katie never failed to be enchanted by the small city which held so much attraction. After coffee and teacakes, in a restaurant opposite the cathedral, they had a leisurely tour of the cathedral itself.

'We'll save the castle for another day, Lyall,' Aunt Alice informed him, 'but I wouldn't mind taking a look at some of those antique shops.'

Lyall winked at Katie and she grinned, glad that they had chosen to come here. They mingled with the tourists examining the stained glass windows and the memorial plaque to Charles Dickens.

Aunt Alice seemed tireless, taking them on a tour of the shops and feeding them with little anecdotes remembered from her childhood. Lyall suggested lunch and, as they enjoyed a traditional roast dinner in one of the many charming restaurants in the high street, Alice Mason wiped her chin on her napkin and said, 'I've had a lovely day and it's such a relief to know that Jack is all right.'

They stared at her and, after a pause, Lyall said carefully, 'Have you seen him recently, Mrs Mason?'

She shook her head. 'No, dear, but he gave me such a lovely card and a pot of marguerites for my birthday. He left them on the step. Strange that no-one noticed him.'

Lyall's face was expressionless.

'When exactly was this?'

'Why, it must have been early this morning because it was there when I opened the door to get the milk. It must have been Jack because most people would have come to the front, but I do wish he'd called in person. I'm not cross with him, not any more. Just concerned for his welfare.'

After lunch, they left Aunt Alice having a rest on a bench in the castle grounds and went for a short stroll. It was bracing by the river. Lyall took her arm and it felt comforting and secure. 'What do you make of what Mrs Mason has just told us about Jack?'

She shook her head. 'Either he's feeling too ashamed to face Aunt Alice or else he's in deep trouble and can't risk being seen.'

'Actually, I think we ought to warn her not to say anything. I feel he could be putting her at risk,' Lyall said.

Katie felt alarmed. 'How do you mean?'

'Well, we haven't any real idea of

what Jack might have got himself into, have we?'

She shook her head. The day, which had started so well, had suddenly taken a downward spiral. She shivered and he turned to her, concern in his hazel eyes.

'It'll be all right, Katie, you'll see!' And he dropped a light kiss on her surprised mouth, leaving her emotions in turmoil.

7

'I'm enjoying working with Lyall,' Shelley said, as she knotted leather thonging through her pendants. 'The thing is, what d'you reckon will happen when we've finished the exhibition? Will Lyall want to stay or is he just helping us out for a few weeks?'

Katie shrugged. She'd been wondering about this herself and, not for the first time was overcome with feelings of anxiety about the future. 'Look, let's just take one day at a time for now, shall we? I'm grateful to Lyall for helping us get our act together, but all good things come to an end, don't they?'

Shelley nodded and, at that moment, Lyall returned with their lunch.

'Why the long faces?' he demanded. 'Come on girls, tell me what's bugging you!'

They went out into the little court-yard area at the back of the workshop, which with its colourful pots of petunias and nicotiana was an absolute picture. Katie said, 'We were just discussing what would happen after the exhibition, Lyall.'

He grinned at them. 'Is that all? From the expressions on your faces, I thought perhaps Faye and Dylan had given us notice to quit or something! Why don't we just concentrate on getting the exhibition out of the way first?'

They nodded in agreement and he poured some wine.

'So that's okay then, but if you think I'm going to leave the pair of you in the lurch then you can't have formed a very high opinion of me, and surely business relationships have to be based on trust!'

Shelley put down her sandwich. 'Look what happened when we trusted Jack,' she pointed out.

Lyall nodded. 'I realise you've had a raw deal, but you'll just have to believe me when I tell you I've no intention of following in his footsteps and leaving you high and dry.'

And they just had to be content with that. For a few minutes, they ate in companionable silence and then Lyall leant back in his chair.

'I was speaking to my friends, Sylvia and Freddy Finch who live near Sevenoaks, yesterday. They're holding a garden party the Saturday after our exhibition, in aid of a children's charity and wanted to know if we would have a stall.'

Katie glared at him, immediately thinking of Olivia. 'Lyall, you know full well we're working flat out to get enough stuff together for the exhibition. How could you even contemplate such an idea?'

He took a sip of wine. 'I'd say we'd have enough exhibits by the end of this week, which would give us a week spare to get some stuff together, but, of course, if you're not interested . . . '

'I'm going away that weekend,'

Shelley announced. 'But, you're welcome to take my surplus stuff if you
like.'

'It's for charity, Katie,' he reminded
her softly and she coloured, annoyed
that he was making her feel guilty.

'And I'd be the first to support such
an enterprise as a rule, but what exactly
is there of mine left?'

'Then just come to help. I'll have a
couple of dozen pendants, some earrings, cufflinks etc. and if Shelley can
muster up the same. We can always
bring photographs of your jewellery.
Advertise the workshop with some
fliers. It'll be good publicity, you'll see.'

'Wouldn't Olivia want to help?'
Shelley asked mischievously.

Lyall collected up the empty plates
and glasses. 'Oh, Olivia can't make it.
She's meeting up with some university
friends that day. Anyway, I really don't
think it's her scene. So, you see, Katie,
if you don't come with me, I shall be on
my own.'

Katie was tempted to tell him that

he'd just have to get on with it, but suddenly realised how selfish she was being. In the past, she would have been only too happy to have helped out at a fund-raising event. For some reason, Olivia Finch seemed to bring out the very worst in her

'Oh, all right, and I suppose I might manage a few additional items by then.' She got to her feet. 'Well, we'd better not waste any more time if we've only got a week to get this show on the road.'

His eyes danced with amusement and she had a strong feeling that he was fully aware of the reason for her initial reluctance to participate.

When he had gone into the work-shop, Katie turned to Shelley. 'So where are you off to that weekend then?'

Shelley blushed. 'I haven't had the chance to tell you, Katie, but I've met this absolutely gorgeous guy, a mate of my sister's boyfriend. Anyway, we're all going on the Norfolk Broads for the weekend.'

'Good for you. It's about time you had some fun.'

As Katie entered the workshop, she collided with Lyall coming out of the store room. He caught her arm, steadying her and she was acutely conscious of the closeness of his muscular body and the fresh tangy cologne he used. Her heartbeat quickened and muttering something about coffee, she freed herself and fled into the tiny kitchenette, wondering if he were aware of the magnetism too.

She told herself severely that she would need to take herself in hand. She was convinced that so far as Lyall was concerned, the kiss in Rochester had merely been a token of friendship, but, for her, it had meant so much more.

She told herself that she had to face facts. Lyall had stepped in to help them over a difficult patch, but despite his reassurances, he'd probably be off when the mood took him, so it was no good harbouring any romantic notions about him. In the meantime, however, they still needed to think long term if the business was going to survive.

Returning with the coffees, she startled her companions by saying, 'You know, I think as soon as we can, we should think about opening the workshop again to the public, at least for one afternoon a week.'

Shelley and Lyall stared at her. 'So what's suddenly brought this on?' Lyall asked her, at length.

'I was just thinking perhaps it's time to advertise this place a bit more and it's always a good idea to let the public see us actually at work.'

'Hmm, so what exactly had you got in mind?' Shelley asked.

'Well, for a start there are a few village functions lined up and we usually open up on those occasions anyway, but I was thinking of something on a more regular basis so that people begin to know where to find us.'

He laughed. 'You are a lady of contradictions, Katie. First you tell me you don't have time to concentrate on anything other than the exhibition and then, a short while later, here you are full of enthusiasm about opening up to the public.'

Katie helped herself to a ginger cookie. 'Well, we have to have a long-term plan. After all, if we're going to survive then we need to project ourselves!'

Having made her point, she settled at the bench and concentrated on polishing one or two of her more expensive pieces of jewellery by hand. Mostly she used a polishing motor with buffing mops, but for special items like these bracelets, embossed with complicated decorations, she preferred this method.

For a time there was silence, as they each worked on their own individual designs. Lyall was decorating a ceramic necklace with an intricate pattern, whilst Shelley was adding to her range of Limoges enamelling, the delicate colours blending into each other attractively.

★ ★ ★

The next morning, an anxious-looking Aunt Alice arrived on Katie's doorstep, almost as soon as the milkman.

'Whatever's the matter, Aunt Alice?'

'Have you got Sheba with you, by any chance?'

Katie shook her head. 'Fraid not.'

'She didn't come when I called last night and she's not been in for her breakfast this morning. Wherever can she have got to?'

'I'm sure she'll turn up before long, don't you worry.'

But the little cat still hadn't returned by lunchtime and it was looking increasingly likely that she'd either wandered off and got shut in some-where, or was hurt. Lyall had made a few enquiries, but he'd had to go off for an appointment and so, by mid-afternoon, Katie decided to pack away for the day and go in search of the cat herself.

She'd had an idea. On several occasions, she'd seen her go into the woods, in fact the animal had often accompanied Jack and herself for part of the way when they had taken a walk there. As she entered the woods now she began to call, hoping that Sheba might respond, but there was no sign of her.

After a while, Katie had exhausted all the usual paths and was not too keen to explore much further. She was just thinking about turning back when she recognised a narrow track which she dimly remembered led to a derelict cottage.

She made her way along it and, soon scrambled through a gap in the fence, scratching herself on some brambles in the process. A shudder ran down her spine as she surveyed the tumbledown place and she realised it had been a stupid idea to come here.

She was just about to retrace her steps when a sudden movement at a window attracted her attention. She whistled and, a moment or two later the door was cautiously opened and Jack stood there — Sheba in his arms. Katie was shocked at his appearance. He looked thinner and was unkempt.

'I might have known you'd suss me out sooner or later!'

'I was looking for Sheba. Aunt Alice is going spare. What on earth are you doing here, Jack? You've worried us all so much. Can I come in?'

'You won't like it. It's not exactly the Ritz.' He stood aside and Sheba jumped down, purring loudly.

Katie looked in disgust at the dirty room with its piles of rubbish. 'However have you managed? This is no better than a pig sty. Come on, Jack, this is ridiculous! Come back home with me now. We can sort out whatever it is that's causing you so much grief.'

'Has Lyall Travis gone away?' Jack demanded.

She shook her head. 'Whatever is it with the pair of you?'

'It's better you don't know. Anyway, that's the least of my worries just now. I suppose you haven't got any food on you?'

'Just some nibbles — a chocolate bar and an apple.'

He stuffed some chocolate into his mouth ravenously.

'How on earth could Lyall let you stay in such appalling conditions?'

Jack was busy brewing tea, boiling up some water on a small spirit stove. 'He doesn't know where I'm staying. He was good to me in the past, Katie, and I know I've disappointed him. He trusted me and I've let him down big time. Everything happened at once. I couldn't cope with it.'

'Don't you think it's about time you came clean about you and Lyall?' She waited with bated breath, bracing herself for the truth, however unpleasant it might be.

He handed her a mug of tea. 'Believe me you wouldn't want to know about my past, Katie. There's a lot of history, things I'm not proud of. Lyall took me in when I was destitute and I've abused that trust. When he turned up in Lyndhurst, I didn't know what to do at first. He tried to persuade me to stay and I said I'd have to think about it.'

She looked at him in bewilderment. 'But I don't understand. Why would you have to leave just because Lyall had turned up?'

For a while he sat cupping his hands round the mug staring into space and then, at length, he said, 'It's complicated because it involves someone else besides Lyall. Please just bear with me for a bit longer, Katie. I'm plucking up the courage to try to put it right.'

She tried another tack. 'But you didn't go away immediately, did you?'

'No. That weekend I went up to London and looked up some mates of mine. We had a wild time, partied — spent a lot of money. They planned to break into an off licence — more for a dare than anything else and asked me to keep a look-out, but I chickened out and came back here.'

If it hadn't been so serious the pun would have been funny. 'Go on,' she urged.

'Round about that time I got some news I'd been waiting for — about some friends of mine I'd lost touch with. They're living in Ireland. I decided to go and see them and make a fresh start. I went to Lyall, asked him to lend me some money, said I'd make myself scarce, but he refused and said I should wait until after the exhibition. Gave me a lecture about loyalty.'

'So that's when you helped yourself to the money?'

He couldn't meet her eyes. 'You've no idea how bad I feel about that but, at the time, I was desperate to get away and Ireland seemed as good a place to go as any. The thing is, I'd let slide to my so-called mates where I was living and guessed they'd follow me down here sooner or later and cause trouble. I realised I'd ruined my chances here and let you all down, but it was too late so I thought it best to go right away.'

Katie was trying to get her head round all this. Jack looked so immature, so boyish and helpless. She wanted to believe him and to make sense of what he was telling her, but there were still so many unanswered questions.

'Oh, Jack, what are we going to do with you? And did you know the workshop was broken into? Obviously those mates of yours.'

He looked genuinely shocked. 'No! When was this?'

She told him briefly what had happened. 'So did you get to Ireland?'

He nodded. 'For a few days, but it didn't work out as I'd hoped so I came back here. As soon as I can I'll move on. It was good here whilst it lasted, but I'm a bit of a rolling stone.'

'So what did you do with all that money you took? You told me, on the phone, that it was to pay off a debt, now you're saying it was to finance your trip to Ireland.'

'I used some of it for Ireland and the rest to pay off a long overdue debt and to help out a friend who was down on his luck. Now I'm afraid I'm virtually skint again, but I'll pay you back as soon as I can, I swear.'

Katie got to her feet. It was obvious they weren't going to sort things out that afternoon and, besides, she'd had enough of being in the cottage.

'Look, let's go and see Lyall, see if we can straighten out this mess you've got yourself into.'

He shook his head vehemently. 'No. I've had too many chances. I should never have got involved with those guys again. I need some space, Katie.'

Katie practically lost patience. 'And what about us, Jack? Come on, don't you think we deserve some sort of explanation for your behaviour?'

Seeing his drawn, pale face she relented and said softly, 'Come on, Jack. I thought we were supposed to be friends.'

He held his head in his hands and said in a low voice, 'Lyall's been a wonderful friend to me, too. I met him a few years ago when I was staying in a hostel where he was doing voluntary work. I'd got in with the wrong crowd and was a bit of a no-hoper 'til he came along. He recognised I had some talent for pottery and encouraged me to develop it.'

He paused. Katie was listening intently, a sudden tide of relief washed over her as he confirmed that Lyall wasn't responsible for driving him away. 'Everything was going well. Lyall helped me find some work, even let me share his flat until I got back on my feet, but then he told me he was going to Australia for about a year and had to rent out his flat. He said I could stay on until the new tenants arrived, and then I'd have to find myself somewhere else to live. That's when I . . . '

He looked up, his eyes bleak. 'It's no good. I can't tell you the rest, Katie, not yet.'

Katie sighed. 'Jack you disappoint me! OK, if you're not prepared to tell me anything else then just explain why you sold Aunt Alice's cigarette box.'

He looked shamefaced. 'I didn't. One

of my mates pinched it off me when I was asleep. I wouldn't have sold it for the world. I just wanted something as a keepsake.'

She didn't know whether to believe him or not. 'There's something else I don't understand. Why did you come back here again after all that had happened?'

'Two reasons. One, I wanted to put things right with you all, but I'm finding that more difficult than I'd expected.'

'And the other?' she prompted gently.

'Aunt Alice has got some papers and other things of mine in her safe. My passport, birth certificate etc. I'd forgotten about them, but now I need them back. If you could ask her?'

'No way! If you want them then you'll just have to ask her for them yourself.'

A few minutes later she scooped up Sheba, promised to keep in touch and left.

★ ★ ★

Aunt Alice was tearful at being reunited with the cat. Katie decided not to mention her encounter with Jack for the time being and said she'd found her near the woods, obviously having been locked in somewhere.

She met Lyall in the lane and told him she'd seen Jack, giving him a watered down version of events. He accompanied her home and came inside.

'So where exactly is Jack now?'

'I'd rather not tell you that for the moment. He's in a dreadful state and I don't want him to take off again.'

Lyall frowned. 'I knew when Jack's e-mails ceased whilst I was abroad, that things had deteriorated, but didn't know quite what to expect when I returned to England. Certainly not this. Perhaps you can persuade him to meet me somewhere. Here, maybe. Jack has a habit of running away from awkward situations, but he's a survivor, Katie, and, after all, he's considerably better off than when I first knew him. He's got a change of clothing, a little cash and transport.'

'Transport?' she queried, puzzled.

'Yes, he nicked Aunt Alice's old push bike. Didn't she tell you? Just between you and me, she was glad to be rid of it!'

He caught her eye and suddenly they burst out laughing and the tension was gone, but there were still things bothering her.

'Why won't either of you tell me what it was he did. Surely it can't have been that bad?'

'It's Jack's story and he must tell you himself when he's ready, Katie.'

'OK, and was it really a coincidence that you turned up here in Lyndhurst or did you come looking for him? Why should I trust you any more than Jack? I've known him longer than I've known you and, until this happened, we were getting on just fine.'

For an answer, he pulled her to him and planted a kiss on her protesting lips. It sent shock waves through her.

'I appreciate that trust has to be earned, and hope I'll soon have done that. I promise I'll speak with Jack and try to sort things out one final time, but, at the end of the day, it's down to him, Katie. Now, regretfully, I must leave you because I've got a dinner engagement.'

She ought to be used to him playing havoc with her emotions by now, she told herself bitterly. She supposed he was going out with the sultry Olivia.

After a solitary supper, Katie went to see Dylan and Faye to ask their advice about Jack.

'It's odd, isn't it?' Faye mused. 'It's almost as if Jack wanted to be found, otherwise why would he hang around here?'

Dylan, always level-headed, suggested, 'Why don't we speak to Aunt Alice and persuade her to look through Jack's possessions to see if there's anything of significance.'

Katie shook her head. 'I don't care what he's done, Dylan. I just want to help him and persuade him to come home.'

The following morning, Shelley startled her friends by announcing. 'Jack's back in the vicinity. Kevin saw him at the farm-shop.'

They filled her in and, after a bit, she put down the brooch she was working on. 'If he comes back here, I'm going to find it hard to forgive him.'

'Well, I for one don't intend to give up on him,' Katie said and, picking up her jeweller's hammer, began to flatten a piece of metal, releasing some of her pent-up feelings.

By the end of the afternoon, she had finished most of the exhibition work and turned her attention to making a few items for the Finches' garden party.

Because of the time factor, she knew they would have to be simple, just examples of what she could do.

That evening, she was tempted to go to see Jack again but decided to leave it for a couple of days to give him time to think things through. She had just returned to Lavender Cottage when Lyall turned up.

'How about coming out to dinner with me tonight?'

She stared at him, taken unawares. 'I've already got my dinner — lamb chops.'

He sniffed, 'but you haven't cooked them, have you? Come on, we can make it partly business and discuss the arrangements for Saturday week and the exhibition too, if you like.'

Reluctantly, she agreed and, soon they were sitting outside a restaurant by a river, savouring the evening sunshine.

For a while, he discussed the charity function at the Finches'. Apparently they'd been friends of his family for many years and he'd looked them up on his return to England, having met up with their niece recently in Australia.

Over dessert, he turned the conversation back to herself. 'So have you thought about your long-term plans for the workshop?'

She spooned up the last mouthful of hazelnut meringue. 'Not yet. We're just taking each month as it comes and not looking too far ahead. We've had one or two quite successful projects and the London exhibition is probably the most ambitious so far. We'd naturally like our little enterprise to become such a success that we can expand, but Shelley and I just love being creative and, until recently, we were actually beginning to see a small profit margin.'

'So now you ought to be looking long term for a healthy profit margin. Anyway, we'll see what transpires after the exhibition, shall we?'

She longed to ask him what his future plans were, but something made her hold back. They lingered over coffee, talking about the theatre and music. When he saw her into the cottage he gave her a light kiss which filled her with longing.

To Katie's relief, Jack was still at the cottage when she called the following afternoon.

'I've made some decisions,' he told her. 'I just needed a bit of space, to clear my head. I recognise what a fool I've been, but now I'm prepared to face up to what I've done and try to put matters right. I need to talk to Aunt Alice alone and try to explain things.'

He sounded so genuine — so remorseful. Katie thought hard for a moment. 'Supposing I told you Lyall's going to be away for most of Saturday and Shelley and I will be at the workshop from mid-morning onwards? I could have a word with Aunt Alice and tell her to be on the lookout for you.'

Hoping she was making the right decision, Katie told him she'd go and see Aunt Alice straight away. Realising there was something else she could do first, she marched off to the café to have a word with Dylan. He listened intently as she outlined her plan.

He rubbed his chin. 'So you'd like me to go round to Aunt Alice's and be there when Jack arrives, but to keep out of the way? You wouldn't ask me to do this if you weren't just a bit worried about what might happen, would you?'

Katie swallowed. 'Perhaps it was a mistake to have suggested it. I don't want Aunt Alice to be upset. She's had enough problems, as it is, without anything else happening. I'd feel responsible if, if anything went wrong.'

'And you've absolutely no idea what it is Jack wants to say to her?'

'No. Only that he wants to speak to her on his own.'

Dylan poured her a large coffee and then went to discuss things with Faye who was in the kitchen. When he returned he said briskly, 'Look, how about I have a word with Aunt Alice now and find out if she's happy about seeing Jack. I'll explain I'll be around in case of any problem.'

Katie felt as if a great weight had been lifted from her. 'Oh, that would be such a relief, Dylan.'

Aunt Alice seemed puzzled by all the fuss, but agreed. She suggested he stayed in the back room within an earshot, although she couldn't imagine that Jack would pose any threat.

At around one o'clock on Saturday, Dylan put in an appearance. 'Mission accomplished successfully,' he informed them.

'Oh, thank goodness! Is he coming back to the flat?' Katie asked.

'Not yet. He realises he needs to talk to the rest of us before then. He wasn't aware I was in the cottage and I don't know what he said to Aunt Alice, but she seemed quite happy. I'm afraid that's all I can tell you.'

8

It was early evening when Lyall returned. 'Mrs Mason said I'd find you here. She's told me about Jack's visit. A very admirable lady your Aunt Alice, so where to from there, I wonder?'

Katie shrugged. 'I'm prepared to give him another chance, but he'd have to pay us back and prove his worth.'

Lyall spread his hands. 'Well, we'll just have to wait and see then, won't we? In any case, he's lost his chance of taking part in the exhibition and it'll depend on Dylan and Faye as to whether they let him have the flat back again. I gather he removed one or two items, so he'll have to replace those.'

She shook her head. 'What a mess some people make of their lives!'

Katie saw Aunt Alice at church the following morning and was promptly invited to lunch. 'Lyall's out, so I'll be eating alone if you don't join me.'

'So how did the visit go, yesterday?' she asked her old friend, carefully.

Aunt Alice's face lit up. I intended to tell you over lunch. Jack's OK, a little thinner and very scruffy, needs a haircut and a shave, but other than that he's the same old Jack. Anyway, we had a good old heart to heart and then I had another with Lyall last night. I feel so much happier about things, dear.

'Anyway, I knew most of what Jack had to tell me already. I'd worked it out for myself. Actually, I've got a bone to pick with you, young Katie. You knew where Jack was hiding out all the time didn't you?'

'Oh, so he told you, did he?'

'I ought to have guessed. It was a pretty obvious place. Anyway, I'm glad we've cleared the air.' Aunt Alice sipped her tea.'

Katie set down her cup. There was something she needed to know. 'Did Jack, did he collect the things he needed from you?'

Aunt Alice gave her a knowing glance. 'Yes, as a matter of face he did.'

Katie nodded. 'Well, it's up to him to make good now, although I don't suppose he's got much money left,' she said casually, watching for Aunt Alice's reaction.

'You'll not catch me out like that, Katie Mead! What went on between Jack and I was private business, at least for the time being!'

And Katie had to be content with that. Her attention was temporarily diverted by an oil-painting over the mantelpiece, depicting a tranquil, rural scene.

'I haven't seen that picture before.'

'I fancied a change so Lyall put it up for me. It was painted by Uncle George's mother.'

Katie took herself off to the workshop where she found Shelley already engrossed in her enamelling.

'I thought you'd completed the exhibition work.'

Shelley grinned. 'So did I, but I had a

bit of inspiration and felt in a creative mood. Anyway, we desperately need to replenish our stock, Katie. I've had to do some trail enamelling on my pendants for the shop because that's the easiest. Does Lyall know Jack visited Alice Mason yesterday?'

Katie immersed in outlining a pattern on to a brooch with a scriber, prior to etching, did not look up from her work. 'Yes, I've just been to lunch with Aunt Alice. Tell me, Shelley, how would you really feel about Jack returning here?'

Shelley considered. 'Well, after all the trouble he's caused, he'd have to turn over a new leaf and promise to stay out of things until after the exhibition. Oh, and he'd have to pay back what he owes us before taking a cut of the profits.'

Katie laughed. 'He'll be drawing his old-age pension before he finishes paying off all his debts at this rate!'

'Perhaps he doesn't want to come back. Anyway, Lyall's here now and he's much more reliable,' Shelley said.

Katie said, 'Look, I quite understand how you feel, but Lyall only came to help out on a temporary basis. He'll be off and away when he's ready and then we'll be back to square one again.'

She was desperately trying to be realistic, but the thought of Lyall going away brought a lump to her throat, and she realised she was becoming too fond of him for her own good.

Shelley packed her things away. 'Well, that's me finished for today. I'm off out with Kevin. See you tomorrow, oh, and Katie . . . '

Katie looked up, 'Yes?'

'If we want Lyall to stay then we'll have to tell him so, rather than just waiting until it's too late. If we're not careful we'll lose him and, personally, I don't think you're so indifferent as you care to make out!'

And, with that remark, Shelley went off, leaving Katie to stare after her, open-mouthed.

Suddenly the door opened and Jack stood there. 'Lyall said I'd find you here, Katie. I've come to tell you I'm going away shortly until after the exhibition. I wanted to wish you all the best for it. You've all given me a purpose in life, even though I still go off the rails from time to time. If you'd consider having me back then I promise I'll pay back every penny I've taken from you.'

She nodded gravely. 'OK. We can discuss all that with the others when the time comes.'

He perched on a stool. 'I think it's high time I told you about Lyall, myself and Aunt Alice.'

She finished what she was doing and gave him her full attention. 'When Lyall left for Australia he arranged for a friend to deal with his mail, but the very next morning this official looking letter arrived. I thought it looked important so I opened it.'

He paused for so long that Katie thought he'd changed his mind about telling her, and then he said quietly, 'It was the enquiry from the solicitor about

Aunt Alice's nephew.'

Katie was listening intently now.

'I've done a terrible thing, Katie and I'm lucky Lyall and Aunt Alice haven't turned me in to the police. They've got reason enough. You see, it's Lyall who's Aunt Alice's nephew, not me!'

Katie's head was in a whirl. 'I can't make sense of this. Lyall has a different surname from Aunt Alice so how can he possibly be her husband's nephew?'

'John Mason, Lyall's natural father, died when Lyall was quite young. A couple of years later his mother married James Travis and he adopted Lyall.'

Light slowly dawned. 'So you decided to reply to the solicitor's letter, pretending you were Lyall?'

'Not exactly. It was a big temptation and a golden opportunity to solve my own problems. I took a photocopy of the letter and made a note of Alice Mason's address and then I resealed the envelope marking it, *Gone Away*. Then, a few days later I turned up on her doorstep explaining that I'd had cold feet when I'd first got the letter, but that now I'd had time to think about it, I'd decided to pay her a visit.'

Katie was still trying to make sense of what he was telling her. 'So you're not Jack Mason at all?'

He shook his head. 'My real name's Jack Page. Coincidentally, Lyall's full name is Lyall John Travis-Mason and of course, Jack is a nickname for John, so it was easy for me to say that's what I preferred to be known as nowadays. As proof of identity, besides the solicitor's letter, I showed her a bill with Lyall's name and address on it and a couple of photographs of him as a child with his parents.'

'Very neat, you'd got it all worked out, hadn't you? But what about your age difference? Aunt Alice is no fool and must have realised you looked younger than Lyall would.'

'Yes, that's where I came unstuck, because I'd no idea that Lyall had stayed with her and Uncle George as a child. I knew George Mason had fallen out with Lyall's father, but assumed it had been before Lyall was born.'

Katie glared at him in disgust. 'So you let Aunt Alice believe you were her husband's long lost nephew? I just can't credit you'd stoop so low, Jack. Deceiving an old lady like that! How could you?'

He had the grace to look ashamed. 'Aunt Alice must have sussed me out fairly early on. She's only just told me that she 'phoned Lyall's tenants who put her in touch with one of his friends. For some reason she took pity on me and allowed me to stay and let me think she really believed I was her nephew, even after Lyall arrived. Lyall said it was up to me to tell her what I'd done, but, of course, they'd both actually known for months.

'I know it's difficult for you to understand, but I really wanted to belong. You see I was taken into care as a child and lost touch with my real family. Recently, I traced them through the Salvation Army. They're living in

Ireland now and that's why I needed the money to go to visit them. They'd agreed to see me and, at first, I was over the moon, but then, when we met up, I could tell I wasn't going to fit in and so that's why I came back here. You and the others are the only family I've got now, Katie, and I'm going to miss you all so much if I have to go away for good.'

He studied his hands. 'Aunt Alice has forgiven me and says she likes the idea of having two nephews around and, if only you and the others could find it in your hearts to forgive me too, then I'd be so happy. I know I don't deserve a second chance, but I promise I won't let you down again.'

He gave her a hug and a gentle kiss. She looked over his shoulders just in time to see the back of Lyall moving away from the open door. Now what would he think? He had obviously misconstrued the situation. She could have wept, realising that his opinion of her really mattered.

After Jack had departed, Katie wondered if she should find Lyall and explain things, but why should she need to justify herself? What about Olivia Finch?

She took a lump of clay from the bin and hurled it at the wall. It landed with a splat, narrowly missing Lyall.

'Artistic temperament?' he enquired with raised eyebrows. 'It won't bring him back, you know. That was a touching little scene I witnessed just now. I was almost convinced there was nothing going on between you and Jack. Hopefully, you're not considering walking out on us before the exhibition?'

Katie glowered at him. Some perverse side of her nature made her say, 'Of course not! What do you take me for? Jack's prepared to wait for me. Now, if you'll excuse me, I want to lock up and you're standing in my way.'

Lyall looked as if he were about to say something else, but, instead, changed his mind and marched off to his car. She sighed, feeling as if she'd just thrown away any chance she might have had of getting closer to him.

For a while, she hadn't trusted him, but now the boot was on the other foot and it was obvious he didn't trust her. Well, if he chose to jump to conclusions without waiting for an explanation, then why should she bother to correct his mistake?

She had a restless night trying to come to terms with her emotions, knowing that she must keep them in check, for Lyall was obviously involved with Olivia Finch. Anyway, she had to accept that he would probably be moving on, once the exhibition was over, and must have no idea of the way she felt about him.

When she arrived at the workshop the following morning, it was to find a message from Lyall saying he wouldn't be in until late, due to some unexpected business he had to attend to.

'Shades of Jack,' Shelley commented when she arrived presently.

It was, in fact, two o'clock when Lyall

finally put in an appearance.

He removed his jacket and hung it on a hook. 'So how are we doing?'

'We are doing just fine. So what kept you?' Katie enquired crossly.

He collected his things together. 'As a matter of fact, I've been up to London with Jack.'

Shelley looked up from her enamelling. 'Oh, so he's finally decided to leave, has he?'

'Where's he gone?' Katie asked.

'I've taken him to a hostel run by a friend of mine. He'll be all right there. Hopefully, it's only a temporary measure until after the exhibition.'

Over tea they discussed the final arrangements for the exhibition, but, for once, Katie's heart wasn't in it. She kept thinking about Jack and wondering if he really would return to Lyndhurst after the exhibition.

'He'll be OK,' Lyall said softly, as Shelley went to rinse the mugs. 'He's a survivor and quite capable of taking care of himself, as you're aware. I gather he's told you about the tangle he got into?'

'Yes, and about you being Uncle George's real nephew. Why didn't you tell me before, Lyall? It would have saved a lot of speculation and mistrust on my part.'

He came to sit beside her. 'Because, if you are to remember, Jack disappeared! Both Aunt Alice and myself agreed it was his story, and that if and when he came back then he had to face up to facts and admit to what he'd done.'

'And was it just chance that brought you to Lyndhurst?'

He shook his head. 'My tenants gave Aunt Alice a friend's number. After they'd spoken, he contacted me. I wrote to her from Australia and told her I'd visit on my return and she must do what she thought best regarding Jack. When she replied she said she'd decided to let him stay on for a bit.

'When I got back to England I was convinced Jack would have moved on

174

and I was amazed to find him still here and apparently settled. You know the rest. I keep thinking that if only I'd loaned him the money, when he'd asked, things would have turned out differently.'

'No, Lyall, you mustn't blame yourself. Jack would have still left us in the lurch — probably taken his own things with him. We've valued your help these past weeks.'

He grinned. 'Thanks for that. Oh, and Katie, I'm aware I got the wrong end of the stick, yesterday. Jack's told me you've only ever had a platonic relationship with him and that he's not got a girlfriend at present.

He caught her hands between his. 'Friends again?'

She nodded, wishing with all her heart that it could be more than that.

The rest of the week flew by. It seemed to Katie that a great deal hinged on the exhibition. She could only hope and pray that it would prove to be worth all the hard work and aggravation on the day.

They set things up on the Friday evening and, when they had finished, Katie had to admit that their stand looked very professional.

★ ★ ★

The following day was busy, but rewarding. A lot of interest was generated in their stand and they took several orders and made a number of sales. They also collected a silver medal for their jewellery.

Around the middle of the afternoon, they had an unexpected visit from Olivia Finch who was accompanied by a tall, sandy-haired young man.

'I've dragged Toby along because I've told him we must support you. He's looking for a present for his grandmother's birthday.'

To Shelley's delight, Toby purchased a cloisonné egg which she had only taken back from Faye and Dylan's shop at the last moment. As Olivia reached out to pick up a brooch, Katie saw the enormous emerald and diamond engagement ring and her heart did a flip.

'Congratulations are in order. Olivia and Toby have just got engaged,' Lyall said in a matter-of-fact tone.

As they left, Katie said, 'I'm so sorry, Lyall, you must be very disappointed.'

He looked at her in astonishment. 'Olivia and I are old friends, nothing more, Katie. She met Toby in Australia. He turned up in England about a week or so ago and asked her to marry him. His father's a millionaire, apparently.'

He frowned. 'Don't tell me you thought that Olivia and I? I only took her out because the poor girl was devastated at parting from Toby and needed cheering up!'

'Thank goodness for that,' Shelley said. 'She's most definitely not your type!'

By the end of the day they were tired but exhilarated at the same time. Kevin arrived to collect Shelley and as they were packing up Lyall said, 'I thought we deserved a treat, after all our hard work so I've booked us a ride on the London Eye.'

It was an experience Katie would never forget, standing with Lyall by her side in a glass pod, his arm around her shoulder, exclaiming over the spectacular views.

As they touched ground again, the others went off to enjoy the rest of the evening. Lyall took Katie's arm and together they strolled along by the river.

'I'm glad today was a success.'

'So am I. Thank you, Lyall, for helping us out.'

There was still something she needed to know. 'Lyall, I've been wondering. What was the cause of the quarrel between your father and Uncle George?'

He looked surprised. 'Didn't Aunt Alice tell you? It was about that painting hanging over her mantelpiece. My grandmother, Josephine Mason, made quite a name for herself as an artist in her day, but she only kept that one picture. When she died both brothers laid claim to it. My father being the oldest won and I inherited it.'

'And now you've given it to Aunt Alice.'

'I brought it with me so that I could produce it when the time was right. You see, Jack didn't know the reason for the quarrel, but I did, so Aunt Alice knew that I was genuine.'

She nodded her head. 'Oh, you're genuine all right, Lyall Travis. I don't know why I ever doubted you.'

Suddenly a lump rose in her throat. 'I suppose you'll be leaving us soon?'

He smiled down at her. 'Well now, that rather depends . . . '

'On what?' she asked rather breathlessly, heart pounding.

'On whether you agree to becoming my wife.'

For a moment she thought she couldn't have heard him correctly, but then he caught her in his arms and kissed her with an intensity that sent the blood pounding through her veins.

We do hope that you have enjoyed reading this large print book.

Did you know that all of our titles are available for purchase?

We publish a wide range of high quality large print books including:
Romances, Mysteries, Classics
General Fiction
Non Fiction and Westerns

Special interest titles available in large print are:
The Little Oxford Dictionary
Music Book, Song Book
Hymn Book, Service Book

Also available from us courtesy of Oxford University Press:
Young Readers' Dictionary
(large print edition)
Young Readers' Thesaurus
(large print edition)

For further information or a free brochure, please contact us at:
Ulverscroft Large Print Books Ltd.,
The Green, Bradgate Road, Anstey,
Leicester, LE7 7FU, England.
Tel: (00 44) **0116 236 4325**
Fax: (00 44) **0116 234 0205**

Other titles in the
Linford Romance Library:

JUST A SUMMER ROMANCE

Karen Abbott

When Lysette Dupont decides to help her grandfather restore his old windmill on Ile d'Oléron off the west coast of France, she doesn't want to get sidetracked into pursuing a deepening interest in the bohemian artist Xavier Monsigny. Xavier has planned to spend his time on the island painting and sketching — but intrigue and danger draw them into a summer romance . . . for, surely, that is all it will be?

A FAMILY SECRET

Jo James

Symons Hill is a charming, close-knit Australian town, where April Stewart's happiness is linked to Symon Andrews of the area's pioneering family. When he leaves suddenly for the city, rumours abound. Heartbroken, April immerses herself in her animal refuge work until he returns unexpectedly. Though he reawakens her feelings, his actions threaten to change the relaxed character of Symons Hill. What has happened to change this once warm, thoughtful man, and how will April learn the truth?

BECAUSE OF YOU

Catherine Brant

Kay Ballard, a primary school teacher, obtained a position as companion to the children of Simon Nash, the composer . . . But at Ashleigh, Kay discovered that the composer's home and background were surrounded by mystery. Three years earlier Simon Nash's wife had died in peculiar circumstances, out of which rumour had sprung and flourished . . . How much of the rumour was false, and how much based on fact, became an obsession with Kay. And when the mystery was explained, danger and tragedy were in the air once more.

STAR ATTRACTION

Angela Dracup

To be on tour with Leon Ferrar should be a dream come true, but for Suzy Grey, his assistant, it becomes a nightmare when she finds herself in love with him. Leon is surrounded by beautiful women, from the voluptuous Toni Wells to pianist Angelina Frascana. Leon and Angelina draw close together as they prepare for a concert in Vienna, but Suzy's desperate course of action threatens to ruin her own relationship with Leon for ever.

GLENALLYN'S BRIDE

Mary Cummins

Queen Johanna destroyed the House of Frazer at Dundallon, after the murder of James I. Innes Frazer, step-sister to Sir Archibald, escaped but was captured by a band of beggars. The leader of the beggars, Ruari Stewart, offers her as a bride to Glenallyn. Innes refuses, only to become a servant of the Queen at Edinburgh Castle, where she again meets James Livingstone who was responsible for slaughtering the Frazers. Innes knows that she must find Ruari Stewart, and one day she might become Glenallyn's bride.

TROUBLE IN PARADISE

Georgina Ferrand

There were no clouds on Lisa Meredith's horizon when she approached the Caribbean island of Santa Angelina for a reunion with her father. But bad news greeted her and she realised that Santa Angelina, with its poverty and squalor, was no island paradise . . . More disturbing was the attitude towards Lisa of those around her, and of Dr. Miguel Rodriguez. Amid seething undercurrents of an island on the brink of revolution, Lisa was drawn into a vortex of love and danger.